Red Asscher Series

Living in Fear
Living in Turmoil
Living in War

LIVING IN WAR

P. C. CHINICK

A Russian Hill Press Book
United States • United Kingdom • Australia

Russian Hill Press
The publisher is not responsible for websites or their content that are not owned by the publisher.

Copyright © 2020 by P. C. Chinick

All rights reserved, including the right to reproduce this book or portions thereof in any form whatsoever.

Living in War is a work of historical fiction. Apart from the well-known actual people, events and locales that figure in the narrative, all names, characters, places, and incidences are the products of the author's imagination or are used factiously. Any resemblance to current events or locales, or to living persons, is entirely coincidental.

ISBN: 9781734122084 (softcover)
ISBN: 9781735176314 (e-Book)
Library of Congress Control Number: 2020937754

For Sheryl

LIVING IN WAR

ONE
Chungking, China 1943

ANYA PAVLOVITCH CRUMPLED A PIECE OF PAPER so tight it left fingernail impressions on her palm. "What makes him think I'm the right person for this assignment?" She reread the order.

```
EDMUND R. ATWATER
OFFICE OF WAR INFORMATION
HONOLULU, HAWAII
    ASSIST DOWNED NAVY PILOT.
    U.S. TRANSPORT TO AID YOU.
    MEET AGENT AT DESTINATION.
```

A cool breeze caused loose strands of hair to brush across her face. Anya fingered them back into place. *What about my ring? The only remembrance I have of my parents, thanks to that treacherous assassin Sun. What about what I want? I translate code for OWI.*

Now I've unwittingly become an agent. I need to get out of this line of work.

The roar of the plane engine grew louder at the Chungking airfield. "I know there's a war on, but how much can one woman take?" She watched Mac's plane, an enormous transport that resembled a gray whale, lift off the dirt runway headed for America. "He'd tell me 'buckle up Sister. You have a bumpy road ahead of you.'" She smiled, saluted the plane as it banked left.

I'll tell Mr. Atwater that I respectfully decline the offer. Yeah, that's what I'll do. He'll understand.

MAC LOOKED OUT THE AIRCRAFT WINDOW AS the plane headed west. They were still low enough that he observed Anya on the ground give him a wave. It had been several months since they had arrived in Shanghai. Their mission together started out rocky, but she had proven herself a worthy partner in his estimation.

I hope she's not angry about my suggesting her for the assignment. She needs to believe she's destined for this type of work. The only way to make that happen is to throw her into it—again.

Mac leaned back in his seat. *All I have to look forward to is sitting out the war behind a desk.*

I suppose the snow has melted and all but gone back

home. Summer will be on the horizon. I'm sure the chores have been piling up for my return; remove storm windows, inspect roof, clean gutters, mow lawn. Endless weekends of drudgery. Anya doesn't know how good she has it. I envy her in every possible way.

A TALL, LANKY MAN IN FADED KHAKIS WALKED up to Anya. "I'm Sergeant Walters, ma'am. We've been instructed to escort you south." His youthful jaw sported a spotty scruff.

Promotions must be handed out fast these days.

He handed her an olive drab knapsack.

"What's this?" she said.

"Supplies, ma'am. You'll want them where you're going."

"Where am I off to?"

"The jungle, ma'am." He turned and marched back toward the airfield shack.

Anya tried to put all the pieces together. Her thoughts reeled as to why she had been chosen for this assignment. *I don't know how to rescue anyone, however, I did save Mac's life back in Shanghai. How am I the only one suited for this job?*

Her mind bounced back in time to when she and Guy had rescued Mac after Sun kidnaped and tortured him. The memory of that day caused her chest to tighten. Mac's rescue had lead to the death of Guy, the love of her life. She had also assisted the Shinjing resistance in the rescue of their leader. *Maybe I can do it, but we're talking about the jungle—poisonous critters, biting insects, the hidden enemy. On second thought ...*

The sergeant turned. "Coming, ma'am?" He entered the shack.

Anya hurried her pace. "Can you take me to your commander's office? I need to send a message." She followed him through the shack to the street where a dusty Army Willys-Overland waited for them. They left Chungking and drove south along a rural backroad that snaked through the countryside. The cerulean sky was intensified by the juxtaposition of lush green rice fields alongside tall stocks of brilliant scarlet and white poppies. *"How can something so beautiful be so harmful?"*

It took them over an hour before the sergeant pulled into a gated area monitored by U.S. military police. They passed through the guard checkpoint to a makeshift camp with rows of dark green pyramid tents pitched on tamped down brown grass. Compared to the beauty she had seen earlier, the drabness did not escape her attention.

The sergeant pulled the jeep in front of the largest tent. Anya and Sergeant Walters entered to find a young man hunched over clickety-clacking on a typewriter. World and local area maps hung from a rope that stretched across one side of the tent. The soldier paused from typing and looked up. "What's up, Sarge?"

"The lady needs to send a message."

"The commander is out. You'll have to come back." He returned to his typing.

"Look," Anya picked up the nameplate off his provisional desk, "Corporal Jackson, I need to send a message to the War Department in Honolulu and I must send it now. Got it?"

The corporal squirmed in his chair. His eyes shifted to the sergeant then back to Anya. "I ... I."

"Don't stutter. Just tell me where the radio is."

"Tell her, Corporal," the sergeant said.

The corporal stood up, hands at his side at attention. "Tent three. It's in tent three, ma'am."

Anya half expected him to salute her as she turned and walked out. "Where the heck is tent three?"

"This way, ma'am." They walked on wooden plank sidewalks. A dusty dirt road lay between two rows of identical tents. Hoots and howls followed by several wolf-whistles that erupted from inside a truck as it passed. Anya coughed from the intense combination of rancid motor oil and petrol exhaust. She dismissed the yowls as childish male antics.

"Sorry about that, ma'am," the sergeant said.

She tried to keep up with his fast pace. "Anya.

Please call me Anya."

"Can't ma'am. It's not our way."

"Our way?"

"The Army, ma'am." He halted. "We're here."

Anya heard the hum of the generator outside of tent three. The two entered. A tall black box with several register meters and glowing dials on the front panel eclipsed the room. Next to it, sat a clerk wearing earphones plugged into a small black box. Above the desk hung a poster depicting a scantily clad woman with curvy legs. The clerk tapped a telegraph key. He failed to notice them until he had finished transmitting his Morse code message.

He turned and eyed them warily. "What are you doing in here?"

Sergeant Walters opened his mouth to speak, but Anya blurted out. "I have to send an urgent message to OWI in Honolulu."

"Let me see your authorization."

"I don't have any. I work for Edmund Atwater, the director. It's urgent I communicate with him. Now."

"Sorry, ma'am. There is nothing I can do for you without direct authorization."

The click-clack of footsteps from behind caused Anya to spin around on her heels. A distinguished man with a bit of gray at his temple, light blue eyes, and square chin peered down at her.

The eagle insignia on his collar told her that he was their commander. The sergeant and the desk clerk both immediately stood at attention and held their salutes until the commanding officer acknowledged them.

"What's going on here?" He returned a salute. "At ease."

"Colonel Colson, Sir," Sergeant Waters stood with his feet wide apart and hands clasped behind his back. "Miss Pavlovitch wants to speak to OWI in Honolulu."

"Miss Pavlovitch, are you in the habit of going over heads to get what you want?" the Colonel said.

Anya studied the tall officer who, in her estimation, had an understanding face. "Sorry, Sir, but I must contact my boss."

"What's so important that you have to speak to Honolulu?"

"It's my assignment, Sir. I'm not sure I am the right person."

Colson rubbed his chin. "Maybe we can do one better. Follow me."

She liked this officer. He had an urbane manner with an easy charm. And he was going to give her what she wanted.

The three retreated to the Colonel's tent. They passed Corporal Jackson who continued to type as his eyes trailed them. On the other side of a makeshift curtain sat a cot and footlocker at its end. There was a small metal table beside the cot where a slate blue box rested on it. The colonel opened the box. Inside was a phone handset.

Two knobs—one red the other black—had wires attached that stretched outside the tent. Under the handset was a dial. The Colonel picked up the handset, placed his finger in the last hole identified with the number zero, and turned it clockwise. It made a rat-a-tat sound as it came back around. Anya heard a muffled voice through the receiver.

"Colonel Colson here. Connect me to OWI Honolulu." He paused then hung up. "They will call us back when the call goes through. Could be a few. Let's see." He glanced at his wristwatch. "It's 1:00 p.m. here, 7:00 p.m. yesterday there. He may not be in."

"He'll be there. He works late. No family there," she said.

"Tell me Miss Pavlovitch, what are you doing in China?" Colson said.

"I was shanghaied into assisting an officer, and now I can't seem to get out of this country."

Colson smiled.

The phone box rang several minutes later. Colson answered the call. "Yes, this is him. Is Atwater in?" Colson handed the handset to Anya.

"He's in."

Anya swallowed hard as she accepted the phone. She did not want to disappoint Atwater, but she had to tell him the assignment was too much for her to handle.

TWO

"Mr. Atwater, Anya here." The phone receiver slipped from the sweat on her palm. She readjusted it to her ear. "About your message—I wanted to, that is—Sir, I am not the right person for the job." She clenched her jaw, held her breath, and waited for his response.

"Miss Pavlovitch, I understand your reluctance but you've been asked to undertake a very important mission. It's not that I'm asking you to do anything I haven't asked another woman to do. And there is nobody else at this late date." She heard him sigh. "For hell's sake, the head of the OSS asked for you by name."

Anya let out a breath she had been holding. "For me? Why? How does he know about me?"

"From Commander Macdonald Benson."

"What?"

"While Benson was in the Chungking hospital

recuperating from his injury, he spoke to OSS who reported a friend of his required some assistance. Having worked closely with you these last few months, he suggested that you would be the perfect person to assist."

Anya's knees started to give way. She leaned against the desk for support. *Why would Mac tell him such a thing?* She remembered how he repeatedly told her that she would be good in military intelligence.

"It shouldn't take long and the Commander specifically wanted you to handle the exchange."

"Exchange? The message said rescue."

"For Christ's sake, the dispatcher blundered the message. I wouldn't ask a woman to go out on a rescue mission. This is a simple handoff."

"But Sir—"

"We are counting on you, Miss Pavlovitch."

Atwater's last sentence resonated as her head pounded and her stomach twisted. They were the same words he used to convince her to come to China with Mac. She stood silent for a moment, then realized she would lose the argument, again. She resolved to comply albeit with reservations. "What is it that I am supposed to do?"

"You will meet someone when you arrive at your destination. It will all be explained to you. Godspeed."

"Yes, Sir. Goodbye." Anya handed the receiver back to Colonel Colson.

"It appears that you will be traveling with us after all," Colson said.

Anya hung her head and wrapped her arms over her stomach. "It appears so."

"We move out in two days time at o-eight-hundred hours. The sergeant will show you where you can get something to eat and a place to rest."

"Thank you, Sir." Anya trudged out of the tent.

I wish I were going to find Joe and my ring rather than on assignment in a hot, sweaty jungle.

IN THE MESS TENT THE NEXT MORNING, ANYA SAT across from a doctor and a nurse who were also traveling with the troops, a mix of both American G.I.'s and Chinese Nationalists.

Anya said, "Nurse Temple, where are you headed?" She took a bite of some kind of pink processed meatloaf. The salty coarse texture hit her taste buds. She reacted with instant dislike. Politeness prevented her from spitting it back onto the metal plate.

"Don't like meat?" Temple said.

"It's disgusting. What is it, dog food?"

"SPAM. Some kind of pig meat. Your accent?

Where are you from?"

"I was born in Moscow but immigrated to the United States before the war."

"Uh, I would have taken you for Irish with that red hair. I don't think most of us in this unit have ever been out of the States," Temple said. "Doctor Finkelstein and I travel with the troops in case we're needed."

"Doctor, do you perform surgery in the field?" Anya said. His wire-rimmed eyeglasses reminded her of Joe.

The young doctor flashed a toothy grin. "I'm a dentist," he said. "It seems there's more need for teeth mending than medical assistance here. Although, I do stitch 'em up and set a broken bone now and again. Anything serious, they're transported out."

Anya pushed her food around the plate with her fork. She could not bear to take another bite. "I'm feeling a bit overwhelmed. I think I'll go lie down for a bit. I'll see you later, Miss Temple." The nurse had been gracious and offered an empty cot in her tent.

On her cot, Anya found a folded two-piece green-brown frog-pattern camouflage uniform, helmet and a pair of boots. Stuffed in one of the boots was a can of foot powder. She opened the knapsack given to her earlier and pulled out a

Remington pistol and box of bullets. She liked the feel of the Remington. She recalled when her father would spend hours training her to shoot with all different types of weapons. Next, she pulled out a dark brown bottle with the printed words: 6•2•2 No-Bite, Insect Repellent. Many hours of protection against mosquitoes, biting flies, gnats, fleas, chiggers.

Chiggers? Where the hell am I going?

The next thing she picked up was a pouch labeled quinine pills. The printed directions read: Take one pill a day to prevent malaria. A few boxes of K-rations were also included along with Chesterfield cigarettes. "Don't need those. Rather have a flask of vodka." She put the bag on the floor and fell onto her cot.

THE BUGLE BLEW THE NEXT MORNING. ANYA jumped out of bed. Nurse Temple was already up, showered, and dressed.

"I forgot where I was," Anya said. "That bugle scared the dickens out of me."

"Yeah," Temple said. "It takes some getting used to." She placed a copy of *The Lady in the Lake* she was reading on the cot and stood. "I'm starved. I'll see you at mess."

Anya was hungry, too, but the thought of

canned pink meat made her gag. She headed for the showers with her new uniform in hand. She stood motionless at the sight of the men queued up to use a crude shower stall. Two-by-fours were stacked together in the shape of a box braced by four long posts. A hose slung over the top beam produced a flow of water. She saw the shoulders and knees of a man in the shower stall. Anya scrunched her lips. *Temple got up early to avoid the men. I wish she'd given me a heads up. Maybe she's not so nice.*

She approached the lineup. The men turned and faced her. Her face flushed and radiated heat. The commander walked toward her. The men quickly turned around.

"Good morning, Miss Pavlovitch."

"Morning, Sir."

"By the way, your uniform has a special button." He took her shirt from her arm and flipped open the top of one of the brass buttons like a locket. Inside was a pointer bearing north. "It might help where you are going."

"Thank you, Sir."

"I'm sure the men will be gracious enough to let you go to the head of the line."

Her face grew hotter. "Um, um ... I'm fine at the end, Sir."

"Very well." He walked off to the mess tent. When he was out of earshot, the men all burst out with laughter. Her urge to run away was precluded by her tenacity and desire for a good wash. *Who knows when I'll have another opportunity?*

ANYA WAITED UNTIL THE MEN HAD FINISHED their showers and gone to the mess before she showered. Dressed in her camouflage uniform, she entered the mess tent and lined up for breakfast. Powdered eggs and pink meat were on the menu.

A heavyset private, who appeared much older than the other kids in the unit, slapped a spoonful of scrambled eggs on her plate. He gave her a glare that made her uncomfortable. She put it at the back of her mind and sat next to Nurse Temple who sipped her coffee.

"Have a nice shower?" Temple smiled.

"Yeah, I did." Anya refused to give Temple the satisfaction of having been one-upped by her. She ate her eggs and washed them down with strong black coffee. *No tea in this man's army.*

By eight o'clock on the dot, all the tents and equipment had been loaded onto various army trucks and the convoy headed out. The only things that remained were overflowing latrines.

THREE

Anya's right hip slammed into the truck door as it careened along a steep, treacherous switchback. *One down, several more hairpin turns to go. I only hope breakfast stays put.*

The convoy headed south on the road to Kunming, according to Colson. Sergeant Walters slowly maneuvered the truck down the mountain. Anya appreciated that it took a skilled driver with nerves of iron to navigate the narrow road.

"We're fortunate the rains have ceased for the moment," Walters said. "When wet, the muddy roadway turns into a slippery ice rink."

Doctor Finkelstein and Nurse Temple sat in the back under a canvas-covered top with the medical supplies. Now and then, the truck hit a pothole. Moans from riders in the back were followed by a fist thump on the panel that separated the cab from the bed of the truck. The suspension, if there was one, had sprung, Anya thought.

She glanced over at Walters' young face and imagined Joe. She wondered if he had found Sun and recovered her ring. *I'm impatient to get this assignment behind me so I can link up with Joe.* The last communication she had with him, he was traveling up the Yangtze toward Tibet.

The terrain changed and the road widened once they reached the bottom of the switchback. Both sides of the road grew bamboo thickets that rose higher than an average man's height. They passed an abandoned overturned truck in a ditch—a common occurrence, she was told.

Walters maneuvered the vehicle to the other side of the road to avoid a dust cloud. He lined it up again as they climbed another mountain. At one point, the truck cleared a large rock overhang within inches of the roof. *You also need to have nerves of steel as a passenger.*

The convoy stopped alongside the road at dusk. "Too hazardous to continue in the dark," Walters said, "and with no overhead lighting a truck might careen over the edge."

Anya rubbed her numb bottom as she exited the truck.

The cook served the troops cold beans and

more pink meat. Anya opted for only beans. An uneasiness washed over her as the heavyset cook's assistant studied her every move. He leaned over the cook and said, "Women are like carpets. They last longer if you beat them every now and then."

"That'll be enough of that Private," Walters said.

"Yes, Sergeant." He glared at Anya.

She sat next to Temple as they ate on the truck's tailgate. Walters and the doctor sat on boxes they had unloaded from the truck.

"The cook's assistant, what's his story?" Anya said.

"Stay clear of him," Walters said. "He's a bad seed."

"What do you mean?"

"Don't know his story but I heard he consented to the draft rather than face prison."

"Thanks for the heads up." Anya took a spoonful of beans, chewed and swallowed. "How long have you been in China?"

"The troops have been here for eighteen months. The doc six," Walters said.

"What about you?" Temple turned to Anya.

The sergeant squirmed. She figured he knew it was an inappropriate question given the circumstance. Secrecy forbade her from telling the truth, that she was here to assist a Navy pilot. "I'm writing an article on jungle fighting for Stars and Stripes." She was proud of how quickly the lie came to her.

"Really? My brother works for that agency. Maybe you know him.

Anya's eyes darted around. She had to think fast. "Well, it's an awfully large agency, and I only contribute articles. I'm not on their payroll." She scanned the area to see the others' reactions. They seemed to have swallowed it, she thought.

That night the four slept in the bed of the truck with the canvas rolled down to keep warm. The cab had no insulation and exposure to mountain air could chill a person to the bone. A row of boxes separated the men from the women. However, it did not avert the sound of their snoring.

OVERNIGHT THE CLOUDS HAD ROLLED IN, THE ground lay damp, and the air had a freshness. They passed through a rural community. Anya was amazed to see villagers lined up along the side of the road to cheer them. Later, they passed a man driving a makeshift wagon with two oxen. He had pulled to the side of the roadway. He tipped his cap as the convoy passed.

"They are very accommodating," Anya said.

"They will do anything to help us drive out the Nips," Walters said.

The truck brakes screeched and the vehicle slid to a stop. Anya heard boxes crash and bodies fall onto the floor in the back, followed by harsh language.

"Something's up ahead," the sergeant said. "I'll be right back." He exited the vehicle and headed up the road. Anya stepped out and went to the back to inform the doctor and nurse of the situation.

Sergeant Walters returned. "A truck has a flat. Should be a half an hour. Might want to stretch your legs."

A loud bang erupted up front. Moments later a soldier ran toward them. "There's been a terrible accident," the soldier said. "Doc, we need you."

The doctor grabbed a small black bag from inside the truck and trailed the soldier. Anya, Walters, and Temple tagged behind. At the scene, an unconscious man lay wedged under a heavy vehicle. His arm was pinned under a steel wheel rim. Beside him lay a pool of blood.

U.S. and Nationalist soldiers attempted to lift the truck together. "The commander shouted orders. "Lift on the count of three. One—two—three." The truck rose and two soldiers pulled the man free.

Doctor Finkelstein rushed over to his patient and inspected the man's injuries. "Nurse, get the plasma kit. What happened here?"

"The truck slipped off the jack," Colonel Colson said.

Finkelstein reached into his bag and pulled out a rubber tube, wrapped it around the arm above the wound, and twisted it tight to restrain the bleeding. He applied gauze pads to the open wound. Temple returned with the kit. The doctor stuck the plasma I.V. into the soldier's other arm. Anya chewed on a fingernail.

"He's stable—for now," the doctor said. "Let's get him into a vehicle." Several men hoisted him up and onto a row of boxes inside a truck. "This tourniquet is temporary. We need to get him to a hospital."

"The army is testing a new triage for wounded soldiers," Colson said. "If we can get to a clearing we can radio and have a helicopter waiting."

"We've got maybe an hour or two before it becomes critical, and the chance of him losing the arm increases."

"Jesus." Colson shook his head. "He was a star college baseball player with a promising career in the pros before he got drafted. Do what you can, Doc."

"I'll give him morphine to keep him comfortable," the doctor said. "But we need to hurry." Nurse Temple placed a damp cloth on the patient's head. She wiped a tear that fell on her cheek.

"According to the map," Colson said, "there's a valley between the next range of mountains. There's no radio signal here. We're sort of at the point of no return, so we'll press ahead. I'll send a jeep back to the last town and radio to have a helicopter out of Chungking meet us at the next clearing.

"How long?" the doctor said.

"An hour, maybe more."

"That's about all this kid has."

THE LEAD TRUCK TRANSPORTED THE DOCTOR, nurse, and injured soldier. Anya and Walters followed behind.

"I hate to see someone die from an accident in this war," Walters said.

"I know what you mean," Anya said.

Walters' hands wrapped tight on the top of the steering wheel. The two remained silent until they arrived at the clearing. It had taken, as the colonel said, over an hour.

In the distance, an olive drab helicopter's rotary blades fluttered.

"There's the eggbeater." Walters pointed.

The injured man was loaded into its belly. It revved its engine and the blades accelerated and went airborne. All eyes watched as it flew over the mountain range.

"Do ya think he'll make it, Doc?" Walters said.

Finkelstein placed his hand on the young man's shoulder. "We'll probably never know his fate. It's war and these things seem to be forgotten by the next conflict."

Everyone dragged themselves back to their respective vehicles and carried on. Anya wished she believed in a merciful god and could pray for the wounded man.

FOUR

THE ROAD THEY TRAVELED HAD BEEN RELAtively flat for several miles. The former twists, turns, and narrow lane gave way to a wide roadway within a forested area although they managed to hit a few potholes now and again. Anya slumped in the seat with her knees bent and the soles of her shoes on the dashboard.

"Sergeant Walters, what is your first name?" Anya said.

"Lucas, ma'am."

"Tell me about yourself, Lucas."

"Why?"

"We've been together for several days and I'm curious."

He shrugged. "Like what?"

"How old are you?"

"Nineteen, ma'am."

"What about your family? Your parents? Any siblings?"

"I have five brothers and three sisters. I'm the oldest." He smiled. "They're back in Gary. Gary, Indiana. My father runs a blast furnace in a steel mill. My mom—well—she takes care of everyone."

"What's it like there?"

"Different from the nearest big city, Chicago. That place is riddled with crime. We live in a neighborhood where everybody knows everyone and everyone's business—good or bad. Kids play stickball in the street. In the summer, the fire department turns on the hydrants, and we run through the water to cool ourselves off. Neighbors help one another with food or clothing. Anything that's needed. We're akin to one large family."

"Sounds very American. Do you have someone special back home?"

"Alice." He blushed. "She's my fiancé." Walters reached inside his jacket pocket, pulled out a picture, and handed it to Anya. "She looks a bit like you with red hair, only her eyes are brown, not green."

Anya studied the black and white of a slender girl. She had long, wavy hair and wore a sleeveless tea-length patterned dress cinched at the waist.

"She's lovely." Anya returned the photo.

"Alice is still in school but we plan to get

married. That is—after I finish college. I don't want to end up like my old man in a grimy steel mill."

Anya recalled how she had once wanted a family and children. She was to have married a Russian military man and spend summers in St. Petersburg and winters at the Black Sea. But the revolution exploded and fate put her on a different path.

A sudden churn in her stomach overcame her. "I think I'm going to need to stop again."

"Good timing. The convoy is stopping. I think others have the same issue."

Anya jumped out of the cab and raced into the woods.

Anya buttoned her khakis and headed back to the roadway. She spotted the heavyset cook's assistant leaning against a tree. Smoke curled upward from a cigarette that hung from his lips. She knew in an instant from the expression on his face what he was thinking. Even though in her past life she had fashioned a living by men, never once did she have one force himself upon her.

He approached her like a wolf after prey. His girth blocked her from returning to the road. Instead, she took off and ran farther into the woods. Anya hoped she could outrun him given his obvious lack of conditioning.

A low hanging tree branch scraped across her face. Blood trickled down her cheek. Another limb caught her shirt and slowed her momentum. She heard his breath near as she continued to run dodging trees, logs, and burrows. Her breath became short. She circled and tried to return to the road but he dove for her and caught her foot. She fell face-first into the dirt.

He gasped for breath as his hands clawed at her pants. She felt her hips lift and her bottoms rip away. His arm pressed against her back holding her in place while his other hand pulled on her undergarment. She tried to scream, but he had her chest pressed too hard against the ground for her to release any sound. She tried to free herself.

Suddenly, he released her.

"Are you all right?" a familiar voice said.

She flipped on her back to see Sergeant Walters and Doctor Finkelstein. The doctor held a small log and a wide grin. The private lay unconscious on the ground.

"I got worried when you didn't return," Walters said as he turned away and handed back her pants. "The doc and I came in search of you in case you got lost."

"I'm all right." Anya's voice quivered. She stood and trembled as she put on her khakis. She brushed the dirt from her face and picked leaves out of her hair. Her chin dipped, embarrassed to look anyone in the eye.

"Let's get you back," Walters said. "We'll have the MPs pick him up and return him to where he should have been placed all along—prison. We have no room for his kind in the armed forces."

THE CONVOY TRAVELED FOR SEVERAL HOURS before it stopped around twilight. Tomorrow they would be at the destination where Anya was to meet her contact. The attack had left her shaken but she had a job to do. She forced herself to close the door on it.

"I could kill for a hamburger—I mean beef burger," Anya said. She remembered the government substituted the word due to its German connotation. "My guts can't take another bean. Is that all you men eat in the Army?"

"Pretty much," the doctor said.

"My intestines are going to explode."

"I have something I can give you." He rustled through his black bag and pulled out a small bottle. "Take one of these for the next several days."

"Thanks."

The three sat around a campfire the sergeant had built. They dined on fish the doctor had caught in a nearby stream. Anya was thankful that beans were off the menu.

"As this is your last night with us," the doctor said, "I thought we all could use a nip." He placed his index finger against his lips. He pulled a flask from inside his jacket pocket and handed it to Anya.

"Why, Doc, you've been holding out on us." She took a swig and passed it to the sergeant, who refused to take part.

"For medicinal purposes." The doc winked. His brow furrowed as he leaned in. "Nurse Temple chose to eat with the Colonel. She's become distant with you?"

"She's afraid if she associates with me, after my attack, it may become a signal and others might try to take advantage of her. I will be leaving soon, and she will be the only woman until you reach Kunming. She's simply protecting herself."

"I can't imagine how that guy thought he could get away with such a vile thing," the doctor said.

"We reside in a man's world and in that world it's the woman who is blamed."

Anya leaned against the wheel well of the truck, took another swig, and thought about the prospect of tomorrow—a hot steamy jungle without a breath of wind.

FIVE

Anya was within minutes of reaching the final leg. She was sad to leave the troops but tittle-tattle about her brutal attack had gone around camp, and things were starting to get uncomfortable for her.

The convoy would continue west while she would head south. Unaware of what faced her, fear crept into her consciousness. She pushed it back and convinced herself she was a strong person who could handle anything.

"Anya." Sergeant Walters steered the truck.

"It's taken you only five days to say my name. I'm impressed."

"Yes, ma'am. I … I wanted to tell you that I think you are one of the bravest people I've ever known. To allow yourself abandoned in the middle of nowhere well—that takes enormous courage. I wanted you to know that before we parted."

"Thank you, Lucas. I hope to live up to your certainty about me."

The truck rolled into a small village that lay in a green valley hemmed in by mountain ranges that spiraled up on either side. A river meandered lazily through the center. A few hovels dotted the landscape alongside rice fields.

Brakes screeched as the truck skidded to a halt. The rest of the convoy, trucks and jeeps, passed them. The commander had said his goodbyes last night.

Anya grabbed her knapsack and stepped out of the vehicle. Heads popped up in a nearby field for a moment before returning to their cultivation. She looked for her expected contact, but no one was in sight. The doctor and nurse climbed out from the back of the truck.

She laughed. "I guess it'll be a toss-up as to who gets to sit up front."

"This road is a supply route so you will be able to pick up a ride within the next few days," Walters said. "But I hate to leave you alone."

"My contact will be here shortly."

Anya gave Nurse Temple a hug. Temple did not reciprocate the embrace. Anya did not feel slighted. She embraced Doctor Finkelstein who wished her good fortune. "Thanks for everything, Doc."

"Take those pills once a day, and you won't have any stomach trouble," he said.

"Will do."

Anya embraced Walters. "I think I'll miss you most of all, Scarecrow." She released him.

He whispered, "I suppose Doc is the Tinman and Temple the Cowardly Lion."

Anya smiled. "Keep safe and take care of yourself. You need to return to that fiancé of yours."

"Keep those boots dry. You don't want to get jungle rot," he said.

The three boarded the truck. The doctor took the front seat. Anya waved as the truck drove up and over the next ridge.

A twig snapped. Anya spun around to see a small Chinese man approach. His skin was dark and weathered. He walked stooped over with a long stick to stabilize his balance. He wore a blue tunic and pants that looked two sizes too big. A gray cap sat atop his head. He did not speak or introduce himself. Instead, he waved at her to follow.

Anya tried to speak to him in several different dialects, but he either did not understand or refused to speak. She followed him as he shuffled to the water where a small wooden boat with a makeshift engine strapped to it awaited. He motioned for her to get in. Water mixed with oil sloshed around the bottom. *I'm not certain what will transpire first, sinking or loss of the engine.*

She held onto her knapsack, staggered to the center bench, and sat. The boat rocked as the old man climbed in. He pulled on the motor cable a couple of times before the engine puttered, then he sat and steered the vessel along the muddy river.

THEY IDLED ON THE RIVER FOR HOURS. THE late afternoon sun beat down on them. Now and then, a cloudburst erupted for a few minutes and passed, leaving a humid stickiness. Anya stripped off her khaki jacket to her thin green T-shirt, but even that felt like too much clothing. She removed her bandana, wiped her brow and neck. Air currents from their movement brought some relief from the swelter.

The rustle in the trees let them know they were not alone. Birds chirped, frogs croaked, insects buzzed, and monkeys whooped. A turtle lumbered out of the water onto shore. Vultures circled above. *What is this place?*

They rounded a bend and the old man cut the engine and maneuvered to shore. A woman dressed in a Nationalist's uniform waited for them. Anya spoke to her in Mandarin as she grabbed Anya's bag and assisted her out of the boat.

"I am Mei."

"Are you my contact?" Anya said.

"No. I'll take you to him. It's a two-day journey."

"Where are we headed?"

"The bush." Mei pointed to the thicket that lay ahead.

"Yes, but where exactly?

"There's no exact. It's the jungle."

They launched their trek in silence through a thicket of bamboo and tall palms. Mei used a machete to slice through overgrown vegetation with her right hand leaving her left to catch branches. A troop of monkeys, perched high in the trees, watched them pass. The sunlight faded and the insects began to feed. Anya put on her jacket in defense. Mei pulled some leaves off a bush and handed them to her. "Rub them on your face and neck. It will help prevent them from biting."

Mei stopped as darkness eclipsed the sky. They used a hollowed-out tree for shelter. "Go find wood for a fire. I'll hunt for food." Her tone was coarse, almost rude.

Anya scrounged for twigs. She picked up a small log and turned it over to find white grubs and worms. She dropped it with a yelp and put her hand to her mouth from embarrassment. *God, I hope Mei didn't hear that.*

Anya returned to the campsite. Mei was holding two skewers of translucent meat.

"What is it?"

"Snake." Mei handed them to Anya and built a fire.

A strange scream caused a chill to run up Anya's spine. "What was that?"

"Death." Mei stirred the flames. "Someone's dinner."

Anya looked at the skinned and gutted meat and gulped. She handed it back to Mei who placed them over the coals. After several minutes, she received a skewer. Anya took a small bite of the tough and stringy meat. It tasted better than the pink meat.

"It tastes—actually I don't know what it tastes like." Anya used her fingers to eat the meat. Her mother's voice rang in her head "A lady never allows food to go from hand to mouth. That is what silver is for." She smiled and licked the remnants that lingered on her fingers.

She glanced over at Mei who had a strange expression on her face. She pulled her knife from its casing and came at Anya.

"Turn around," Mei said.

"What?"

"Turn around, slowly."

Anya obeyed. The point of a blade pressed on her upper back. She turned back. On the end of the knife was a hairy golden-colored tarantula. Its long hairy front legs extended toward her.

Anya's knees gave way and she crumpled to the ground. "Tha ... thanks."

Mei stoked the fire then lay on the ground and curled next to it.

Anya was restless, her nerves frayed, and she was not ready for bed. "Where are you from, Mei?"

"Better save your energy for the walk." Mei turned her back to Anya.

Anya tumbled back and rested her head on her knapsack. The image of snakes and insects crawling on her kept her from a restful sleep. She yearned to swing in the trees with the monkeys.

SIX

ANYA AWOKE TO A PUNGENT ODOR. SHE ROLLED over to see Mei squatting, roasting fish over a newly stoked fire. Anya studied the woman. She wished Mei was more of a talker. *Maybe she doesn't get close because she's afraid. It's hard to make friends in war only to lose them later.* Anya pondered about people from her past who were no longer alive.

"Hungry?" Mei said.

"Starved." Anya sat up and rubbed the sleep from her eyes. "What time is it?"

"Morning."

Anya snickered to herself. *Stupid of me to ask. She would tell me there is no time, it's the jungle.* She surmised it was early due to a small degree of low-rising light that pierced through the trees.

"We need to eat and push on ahead of the heat." Mei gave her a friendly smile as she handed Anya a piece of fish.

"You know that's the first time you've been nice to me."

No response.

"Tastes good." Anya refilled her canteen from the stream. Mei doused the fire until the coals were cool enough to pick up and tossed them into the water. She erased any trace of a fire or of them having been there.

Anya picked a long green weed and twisted it in her hands forgetting her surroundings for the moment. She started to hum an old tune. Mei spun around with a red face, her eyes protruded. Anya froze.

Mei whispered, "Do you want to get us killed? Enemy troops patrol this area."

Anya winced. "I'm sorry. I was lost in thoughts." *So much for her being nice.*

Mei turned her back. Anya stuck her tongue out at her. She rethought her actions and bit her lip. *After all, she's trying to keep me alive.*

The heat of the day had taken its toll. Anya's arms became heavy and with the knapsack strapped on her back, each step became harder and harder and harder. The humidity felt more like drowning than breathing. She longed for the rains of Chungking or even the stench of Shanghai over the sweltering rainforest. She heard the high-pitched screeches of exotic birds and the crescendo whoops of monkeys throughout the trees. A troop sprinted ahead from tree to tree, and a company of parrots flew by. *Where in the hell are we going?*

Mei abruptly stopped. A shot rang out. She crouched and motioned for Anya to get down. Another shot whooshed past Anya's head. Mei grabbed Anya's hand and together they headed into a thicket. Mei stood behind a tree and placed her fingers to her lips.

Anya nodded and slipped off the backpack. The bullet had ripped through its side. She knew by the size of the hole that it came from a rifle. The bag had saved her from death. She dug into the duffle and pulled out her pistol. A shot pinged off the bark and a second hit the dirt. Anya assumed it was a single sniper, otherwise there would have been a multitude of simultaneous shots.

Mei signaled to Anya to stay. Mei made a wide circle and crept back to the other side of the path. Bullets continued to crack, whizz, and zip past.

Fear swelled as Anya panicked at the possibility of Mei's death. She had no idea where she was or where she was going. *I could be out here wandering for weeks. I have to help Mei.* Anya failed to notice that the sound of gunfire had ended. She inched her way from behind the tree. A rustle in the bushes caused her to raise and point her gun. A familiar voice called out.

"Don't shoot. It's me."

Mei walked toward her as she wiped a bloodstained knife against her pant leg. Anya declined to ask. She did not want to know. All that mattered was that they were both safe—for now.

They continued along the path, alert to their surroundings. Clouds that had gathered earlier now broke free of their moisture. Anya lifted her face and let the rain wash over her. A chill in the air was a welcome relief.

Anya heard a flutter in the distance. She drew her pistol. Mei gently pushed her hand down. Out of the bush emerged a tall thin Chinese man. He had exaggerated facial features with high cheekbones, bushy eyebrows that hung over wide deep-set eyes. And a wide flat nose with a mouth that stretched halfway across his face. He wore a black top and pants with a wide-brim bamboo hat. A holstered pistol slung over his right shoulder. He sported a wristwatch on his left arm accompanied by a gold wedding band on his finger.

"Miss Pavlovitch." He bowed and spoke to her in English. "I am Loke, your contact."

"American?"

"No. But educated at Berkeley."

Mei spoke to Loke. He translated for Anya. "She said that you ran into a sniper."

"I understood what she said."

Loke's face flushed. "You speak, Mandarin?"

"I lived in Shanghai for several years."

Loke reverted to Mandarin for Mei's sake. "I'm glad you're both all right."

"Mei is very talented with a knife." Anya glanced her way and smiled.

Mei stared at her with a glint in her eye.

"We should go before the enemy sends out a search party."

Anya followed Loke, with Mei close behind. They traveled uphill on an animal's path. They reached the summit and Anya asked to rest. She collapsed on a large boulder, caught her breath, and wiped her brow on her sleeve. Loke and Mei ventured out in search of something edible. Anya scanned the cacophony of greens that painted the jungle canopy below. She imagined what an impressionist painter could do with such beauty.

Mei and Loke returned with berries they had picked. The three sat, ate the fruit, and drank water. Anya enjoyed the cool breeze from the mountaintop. She assumed they would soon return to the scorching heat with swarming mosquitoes, leeches and biting ants.

"How much farther?" Anya said.

Loke's eyes darted over at Mei then pursed his lips at Anya.

"What?"

"We have a problem." Loke paused to clear his throat. "This was supposed to have been an easy handover but there's been a new development."

"Meaning?" Anya said.

"Our ground network discovered that the pilot, after he parachuted from his burning plane was ambushed and is now in the hands of the enemy. Not sure about the rest of the crew."

"And … so?" she said.

"Unfortunately, the mission has gone from hand off to rescue," he said. "I'm sorry but you're apart of it now."

Atwater said he would never send a woman on a rescue mission, but here I am.

SEVEN

ANYA SAT ON A ROCK AT THE TOP OF THE mountain and contemplated how they would rescue a U.S. pilot from the Japanese. She scuffed the dirt with one foot and rubbed the back of her neck. "How many others are there to help?"

"We're it," Loke said.

Anya glanced at Mei and rolled her eyes. "Where is the guerilla army I was told about?"

"Tied up in a battle several miles north of here. They will come when they can. Though, I suspect it may be too late."

"Too late?"

"It's taxing to take on prisoners in this region," Loke said. "They require men to watch and feed them. It takes soldiers away from the fight. It's better to dispose of them."

Mei nodded in agreement.

"How many of the enemy are we talking about?

"A dozen—give or take," Loke said.

"Can we radio for assistance?"

"Radios are useless in these mountains. However—" He paused and scratched his chin. "We could send an LR north with a message."

"LR? Is that some kind of carrier pigeon?" Anya said.

Loke laughed. "We call 'em Little Resisters. They're local children as young as ten. Boys and girls, who help us—harass the enemy. They're small and wiry and can easily elude the Japs who regard them more of a nuisance. They have proven to be very effective. They'd give their lives if asked."

"How often are they asked?" Anya said.

No response, only a blank stare.

"Can we drum up some local farmers?" she said.

"Our forces are comprised of peasants, students, and displaced military people. The only civilians still managing a somewhat normal existence are too frail to walk long distances, let alone carry a rifle."

Anya stood with her hands on her hips. "I don't see how three can defeat a dozen armed soldiers."

"You underestimate us, Miss Pavlovitch." His voice remained calm, almost serene. "We've been at this war since 1937 and we're still kickin'. I think we can manage to eliminate a few soldiers and rescue your pilot."

"I don't mean to insult your abilities but—" Unable to finish her thought, Anya pushed herself off the rock and paced. "Okay—let's say I go along with your proposal. What's the plan?"

Loke said, "We have rifles, grenades, and flamethrowers. Weapons are not an issue. You're concerned about the children?"

Anya nodded.

"The young ones are trained to do all kinds of things," Mei said.

"They are fiercely loyal and want to rid their country of invaders. We don't recruit. They come to us," Loke said. "We'll have them do reconnaissance. They can report on the number of soldiers and how their camp is set up. We're seeking to find vulnerability. We can gain an advantage with a surprise attack. But now, with a half day's journey to reach the stronghold, we need to be on our way."

VINES GRABBED AT THEIR ANKLES AS THEY walked through the jungle. The steamy heat once again sapped Anya's strength. Even the monkeys were silent resting in the trees.

They came to a river the width of six sampans. Tree branches dipped their green-leaf foliage into the stagnant water.

"Is it deep?" Anya said.

"About waist-high," Loke said.

"Are there alligators?"

"None that I'm aware of."

"That's not very reassuring."

"I'll enter first," Loke said. "Mei will bring up the rear."

Anya remembered what Sergeant Walters had said. "Keep your boots dry." She removed her boots, slung them over her shoulder and dipped her foot into the water. The iciness surprised her. She scanned the surface, gulped a breath, and waded in.

The water rose above Anya's waist in the middle of the river. A sudden burning sensation emanated from her leg but she ignored it and persisted. Loke helped her as she reached the other side. She lost her footing on the muddy bank, but he caught her as she fell. He tried to assist Mei, but she lost her footing before he could reach her. She was able to catch herself before she fully submerged.

Anya sat to dry her feet with her socks before

putting on her boots. She pulled her pant leg up to inspect a nagging biting sensation. She let out a scream that caused Loke and Mei to run to her aid.

"Shi Zhi," Mei said.

"What is it? What is it?" Anya tried to slap the slimy sucker off, but it had fastened itself to her leg.

"A leech," Loke said.

"Get it off. Get it off."

"Don't panic. It won't hurt you. They are actually used in many different medicinal ways."

"I don't care. I want this slimy thing off me." She pulled at it.

"Stop," Loke said. "You'll only remove the body not the sucker."

Dizziness overcame Anya and she fell back.

Mei knelt next to her and slid one of her fingernails underneath body to the sucker. It reattached itself to her nail. She carefully removed it and threw it back into the water.

"We'd all better remove our pants and check any part that was in the water," Loke said.

They each, in turn, went behind a bush.

"Nothing here," Loke said.

Mei came out and shook her head.

After several moments of silence, Anya piped up. "I'm good." She walked out from behind the plant. "I guess I'm the only one sweet enough for them," she said with a hesitant chuckle.

Anya's body shuddered now and again at the notion of creepy crawlies stuck to her. She could stab and kill a man, blow up a building, but she drew the line when it came to things attached to her body—eating her.

THEY REACHED THE STRONGHOLD AT TWILIGHT. Pants, shirts, and jackets were pinned together as makeshift tents. An elderly Chinese woman dressed in a long frock stirred something liquid in a black pot that hung over an open fire.

Three children huddled around the campfire holding empty bowls. Two wore caps and the other a bamboo hat slung over her back. They were dressed in black pants and tops with red scarves tied in a square knot. To Anya, they looked like American Boy Scouts with the exception of rifles flung over their shoulders.

Loke greeted the woman and children and introduced them to Anya. "This is Mother Mary and these are our Little Resisters. We call them Huey, Dewey, and Louie. The impish girl on the end prefers the name, Louise. No one knows any one's real name or where they're from in case any of them are captured."

Anya noted that he did not use her name. "It's very nice to meet you." She spotted one of the boys who had a pale yellow snake with black stripes the diameter of a twig wrapped around his arm like a bracelet. Its tongue flickered in and out. *Must be a pet. Hope it's nonvenomous.*

Loke slapped his hands and rubbed them together. "Looks like we're in time for dinner."

"It's rice soup," Mother Mary said. "Grab a bowl."

Anya squatted next to one of the children and looked inside her bowl. *It looks like gray gruel.* She took a sip. *Yum. It's better than it looks.* She continued to drink her meal.

Loke sidled next to Anya. "You look exhausted."

"I've bounced from place to place in this hot jungle, been shot at and had my blood sucked on. What I need now is sleep." Anya lay back and pondered what terror might occur tomorrow. She worried about the children's safety. *The sacrifices we make for country are immeasurable against the personal losses.*

EIGHT

ANYA WOKE TO THE SOUND OF WHOOPING monkeys. She felt rested yet not eager to start the day. Today would be filled with kill, kill, kill, and more killing. She had her fill with death and wanted to find Joe who was helping recover her ring. But her father had drilled her to believe in courage, honor, and duty—most of all, duty.

She wrinkled her nose at a foul odor that permeated her surroundings. It occurred to her after sniffing her armpits that she was the source. It had been days since she had bathed. *If this might be my last day, I want to go out looking my best.* She trotted to the creek and found a deep pool. She hesitated for a moment, worried about leeches then stripped off her clothes, inhaled a deep breath, and dove into the water.

Anya heard a splash and swirled around to find Mei in the water with her. She flashed a rare smile as she swam near. Mei placed her hands on Anya's waist. Anya pushed her away. A flush crossed Mei's face with a downward glance. Anya swam to shore. The event left her puzzled. *Why would Mei be willing to be intimate but not open to conversation? Maybe she saw something in me from my past. I once had an intimate relations with a women when I first lost my parents but that was a lifetime ago.*

At camp, Anya found the children gathered near Loke. He pushed a stick in the dirt and drew a circle. The attentive kids nodded. He addressed them one at a time. Too far away to hear, Anya assumed he gave them each a mission. Together the LRs stood up and left camp.

Anya walked over to Loke. "Will they be all right?"

"Yes. They are small and can easily hide in the brush, providing us with vital information."

"How far is the enemy camp?"

"A good hour there and back. They'll return by early afternoon."

"You don't go with them?"

"They are better on their own. I might compromise their position."

Mei walked past Anya. They avoided eye contact with lowered heads. Loke's brow furrowed. "Is there something going on between you two?"

"No."

"We will be engaged in battle, and I don't want any personal issues to get in the way."

"Everything is fine." She lied.

THE REST OF THE DAY, ANYA REMAINED TENSE. She assisted in preparing weapons, restocking rifles, pistols, and refilling a grenade belt. They had one flamethrower but fuel was low. Images of the Little Resisters entered her mind. They were children to her, but in many ways, their childhood was lost to them. Today they were soldiers fighting an impossible war.

Mei had steered clear of Anya, but Anya was aware of her presence. She did not hold animosity or an uneasiness toward Mei but compassion. The fact that she had given away her secret made her more endearing.

Mei approached Anya. "Can we talk?"

"What's on your mind?"

"Um, I ... didn't mean to scare you earlier. I thought that you were—you know."

"I'm sorry if I gave you that impression. I figured since my life is in your hands, it would be nice if we were friends."

"I'd like that—that is if you still want to."

Anya stuck out her hand. Mei reciprocated with a handshake.

THE RETURN OF THE THREE RESISTERS UNHARMED was a relief to Anya. Loke called an immediate meeting. Everyone had gathered with the exception of Mother Mary who had packed her things earlier. She had been kind enough to leave them one last meal before she headed back to her village.

Louise drew a diagram of the campsite in the dirt. She marked the location of three tents, a food station, and eight soldiers.

"Each soldier has a rifle and one or two grenades hung from their belts," Huey said. "There is a canvas-covered pile of ammunition." He marked it on the diagram. "No vehicles, no visible machine gun, and no sign of others beyond the camp."

Dewey reported a single prisoner was in a pit several yards from the tents. He pointed it out on the drawing. "It's the pilot. I was able to get close enough to toss your written note to him to let him know we would return."

Anya stood stunned at their report. *Grown men could not have done any better.*

"All right everyone. Let's eat then head out." Loke looked at his wristwatch. "In fifteen minutes."

After the meal, everyone broke camp. Anya wrapped a rope several times around her waist and flung her bag on her back. She placed a pistol in her belt, another one inside her boot, and shouldered a rifle. Mei strapped the flamethrower with its metal gasoline container to her back and cinched a grenade belt on her hip. Anya gave her a nod. Loke carried a rifle in one hand, another over his shoulder, and several bullet belts slung over the other shoulder. The Little Resisters followed close behind.

They did not bother to remove any trace of their camp. No one would come back to this location.

NINE

THEY ARRIVED AT THE JAPANESE CAMPSITE WITH enough daylight to see the entire layout. It would be dark soon when they needed to strike. Anya had questioned the use of the children, but Loke assured her they were sharpshooters and would be at a reasonably safe distance. If things went bad, they had orders to retreat.

They hunkered down in the tall brush and monitored movement. Loke crouched in the center, close to the camp. Mei flanked his left and Anya his right. The Little Resisters were perched in trees with their rifles drawn. They would be the first to pick off the enemy on Loke's signal. Mei would ignite the ammo pile. Loke would draw their fire while Anya rescued the pilot.

The layout was exactly as Louise had drawn it. Three dark green tents lined up side by side, backed by a row of trees. The pile of ammo lay in the foreground, a good distance from the tents. The pit that held the pilot was to the right of the farthest tent.

Unlike Anya's frog-pattern camouflage uniform, the enemy wore green with a vine design that blended better with the local vegetation. Their helmets were equipped with green netting, stuffed with twigs and leaves. All eight soldiers were present. Three sat huddled together. One prepared a meal, and the others ambled about.

Loke let out a loud whistle. Enemy heads shifted their way. Three shots rang out from the trees. Each hit its target. The Japanese scurried for cover. Loke dropped another soldier. Mei rushed within a hundred feet of the ammunition pile and released a long fire stream. It ignited the stash, which within moments exploded. The blast lit up the sky, impaled two soldiers with shrapnel, and with a wave knocked Mei on her keister.

Anya dropped her knapsack and skirted to the far side of the camp with a drawn pistol. She hid at the tree line behind the tents. The pit lay straight ahead. She uncoiled the rope about her waist and secured one end to a tree. A Japanese soldier crossed her line of sight. She aimed and pulled the trigger. He jerked. His arms flailed and he fell. Shots flew in all directions. Smoke filled the air. Screams, cries, and moans echoed.

Anya stooped, and with the end of the rope in one hand, crawled to the pit. Flat on her belly, she peered inside. The pilot's eyes reflected hope. A strong ammonia scent wafted up letting her know in an instant that it was the soldier's latrine.

"Lieutenant Jones?" Anya said.

"Yes."

She threw him the rope. "Climb out."

The sound of movement caused Anya to look up. A soldier approached with his fixed bayonet pointed at her. He advanced with crazed eyes and a sinister grin that exposed missing teeth. Her heart pounded harder with each step. A bullet from behind ricocheted near his foot. He advanced. Another shot grazed his upper arm. A third hit the back of his thigh and passed through. He stumbled. He staggered. He advanced. Anya raised her pistol and fired. He halted. A hole in his forehead produced little blood as his knees buckled.

Lieutenant Jones emerged from the pit. He rolled over on his back and caught his breath. His head turned to Anya. His eyes pierced hers with gratitude. Her guts twisted at the sight of him covered in filth, but she was thankful he was alive.

"Are you hurt, Lieutenant?"

"Just wait till I get my hands on those Nips. I'll kill every one of them. Where's my crew?"

"You're the only one here."

Anya realized the fighting had ceased as Loke walked toward her. Mei trailed behind.

Anya scanned the area. Dead bodies sprawled in the dirt. The cook's head and torso hung over a large black pot. A detached arm lay in the dirt. The ammo pile continued to burn.

Loke directed his fingers at his eyes and then pointed them at the camp to signal everyone's need to search for additional soldiers. He combed through each tent looking for anything of importance to take with them.

Anya heard gunshots followed by a small explosion. "What was that?"

Loke exited a tent. "I decommissioned their radio."

"What's that smell?" Mei said as Jones passed.

"Don't ask," Anya said.

"I think they're all dead," Loke said.

"Not quite," Jones said. "There are maybe ten or so unaccounted for. They use this as a base camp. Several go out for a few days and hunt for food and reconnaissance. I say we go find those sons-of-bitches."

Anya piped up. "My orders are to get you back to your unit in one piece and we do not have enough supplies to engage the enemy."

"We may have a half a day before the patrol returns," Jones said.

"I found a map." Loke pulled it out from an inside pocket and unfolded it. "It appears they might be patrolling up north—near where we're headed. We'll have to travel by river. It will be the fastest means to reach safety. Our only worry—we might run into a Jap patrol boat."

Huey and Dewey carried Louise over their shoulders. "She's got a bullet in her backside."

Anya rushed over. She spotted the hole in the clothing. "Why isn't there more blood?"

"The bullet is still lodged. It's probably corking the blood vessel," Jones said.

"Will she be okay?" Anya said.

"If shot, it's the best place." Jones slapped his butt. "Fleshy."

Loke broke off the legs of a cot and placed Louise on her stomach. "You boys carry her to the nearest village and get her medical attention."

"I want to go with you," Huey said.

"You have your orders."

Huey grumbled as he and Dewey carried Louise off.

Loke faced Mei. "Burn everything."

Mei smiled and then torched the tents until the fuel ran out. The entire camp smoldered as they retreated into the jungle.

Anya tripped on a thick vine and fell forward. She caught herself on Jones's back. He turned. "If you wanted to get my attention, all you need to do is whistle."

"Funny." Anya wiped her hands on her pants legs. She lingered until Mei pushed her to move on.

They reached a wide creek. Jones took the opportunity to plunge into a deep pool. Everyone sighed with relief when he emerged less odoriferous. It was the first time she noticed Jones's blond hair and brown eyes. His shabby uniform hung off his bones.

He probably hasn't had a meal in days. I'll bet he could eat a pound of pink meat and a bucket of beans.

"The Japs will soon be on our trail. We need to find a place to hide." Loke said.

TEN

The sun peeked above the horizon as they stumbled upon a small village. It had been a grueling twenty-four hours, and everyone needed food and sleep. Loke arranged a trade with an elderly farmer for food and a place to rest for one of their rifles.

The farmer brought bowls of rice and served each of them. Anya offered Jones her bowl, but he refused. They slept in a dilapidated A-framed wooden structure that was once a house.

Anya heard the snores from Jones as she lay her head on her bag. She thought about what the next several days might bring. Her hope and foremost challenge was getting the lieutenant home safe without another incident.

Anya felt a tug on her shoulder. Someone whispered in her ear. "Wake up. Wake up." She rolled over. Her brow furrowed at Mei's wide-eyed expression. Fear rolled across Mei's face. Anya heard unrecognizable voices emanate from outside. She sat up. Her arm hairs bristled.

"Soldiers." Mei pressed her finger to her lips.

Anya jumped to her feet and peered between cracks in the wooden wallboards and listened. There were three of them. One grabbed the farmer by his shirt and shook him like a limp ragdoll. He demanded food and water. A pang tore throughout her body. She hoped the farmer had not given them the last of their food. Anya knew soldiers could be ruthless if they did not get what they wanted.

A squeak emanated from the back door. Footsteps shuffled toward them. All heads turned. Loke raised his weapon. The farmer's wife, a matronly woman, appeared in the doorway. In her hand was the rifle they had exchanged for room and board. Everyone froze.

The matronly woman motioned for them to follow. She ushered them into the cobwebbed kitchen. The floor had not seen a broom in years. Dust kicked up as she pushed an oversized hutch to one side. Behind it, the wall had been cut out. Anya figured they were not the first to use this hideout. The space appeared too small to accommodate all four. Mei and Anya went in first followed by the men. They squeezed in and lined up in a face to back fashion. The old woman handed the rifle to Loke. "We will all be shot if they discover we have a weapon." She secured the hutch.

Anya could feel Jones's hot breath on her neck. She held in a hard sneeze that hurt all the way to her toes. The air grew stale. Her breath increased. Her heart rate accelerated. Perspiration dripped from her temples and the nape of her neck. She prayed the soldiers would leave before they all fainted.

Heavy footsteps entered the kitchen. Anya's muscles stiffened. Her mind snapped to attention. *Oh, God. I forgot my bag.* Her knees buckled, but the pressure of the other two bodies held her upright. She hoped the farmer's wife had hidden it.

The clomp, clomp, clomp of footsteps resounded throughout the house. There was a crash—shatter—moan. Anya flinched. A voice from inside the house yelled. A commotion filled the house. More yelling. A slap. A shot. A thud. Anya tightened her grip on Mei's shoulder. Mei recoiled and Anya released her hold. More footsteps, a door slammed, and then silence.

THE HOURS CREPT BY AT A FUNERAL'S PACE. Someone eventually slid the hutch to the side, exposing daylight. They stumbled out from their hiding place. A figure stood in front of Anya, but she could not discern if it were friend or foe. Her eyes adjusted to the bright light. The farmer's wife wiped her tears with her dingy apron.

"What happened?" Anya said.

The wife pointed to the next room. Anya walked over to the farmer, lying on the floor. His head lay in a pool of blood. Eyes remained open. Her knapsack lay beside him. Anya put her hand to her mouth. She stared at the dead man with a lump in her throat.

His eyes are staring at me, into me, through me. What have I done?

The farmer's wife picked up the knapsack and gave it to Anya. She wanted to embrace her but knew the Chinese culture deemed it unsuitable for a stranger to hug another. Instead, Anya walked into the other room. She stood for a moment, threw the knapsack, and collapsed in tears.

Mei knelt to console her. "It's my fault," Anya said. "If I hadn't forgotten the bag, he would still be alive."

"No one is blaming you," Loke said. "She understands these are the costs of war."

"I'm blaming me." Anya wiped her nose on her sleeve. "The least we can do is provide a proper burial."

Lieutenant Jones approached the body. Loke held up his hand. "Don't disturb him. If we move him, they will know we were here."

"We can't leave him," Anya said.

"That was a scouting party. Their unit is probably nearby. The best thing we can do for her is to leave before they return."

"If they return they will kill her. We should take her with us."

"She won't come," Loke said. "Besides, she's already gone to the village to find someone to take her in."

Mei helped Anya off the floor. "We need to go."

Jones passed Anya her bag. She slapped it away. He picked it up and threw it over his shoulder.

"Try to step in the footprint of the person in front of you," Loke said as they left the farm. "That way the enemy won't know our numbers." He led the way. Jones and Anya followed in single file. Mei bought up the rear.

They descended into the jungle to avoid future contact with other villagers and farmers. Anya tried to push the ugliness from her mind. The farmer would not be the last to die in this war, but she would never forget him.

ELEVEN
Washington D.C.

MAC NESTLED THE PHONE RECEIVER BETWEEN his chin and shoulder. "This is Commander Benson." He rubbed his upper left arm where Sun's bullet had ripped through the triceps tendon. Although healed, it still ached with an occasional tingling in his fingers.

"Hold a moment. Edmund Atwater would like to speak with you." Mac stared out the window of his office. He had a splendid view of the Capitol Building. The only thing about his new assignment that he favored. He longed for field duty but promised his wife Helen he would take a desk job to salvage their marriage.

Mac glanced at the clock on the wall. The hands pointed to 4:47. *Is this what my life has come to? Waiting for five o'clock to go home, have dinner, only to get up and do it all again the next day.*

Mac heard a voice over the phone.

"Commander, Atwater here."

"Yes."

"I thought you should know since you and Miss Pavlovitch had spent time together in the Far East.

"Yes."

"I'm sorry to tell you this, but she's missing in action."

Mac gripped the receiver tight and leaned forward. "Missing?"

"She was to pick up her assignment and deliver it to Kunming, but there was some trouble and—well—we don't know what happened."

Mac's mind flashed back to Shanghai. He had been in a confused state as his eyes opened. Anya hovered over him. Her furrowed brow alerted him that something had happened.

"Glad to see you back among the living," Anya said.

Mac struggled to get the words out "Where—where am I?"

"A friend's flat. It took some time to find you and when we did, you were in bad shape. Sun did a pretty good number on you."

"How long?"

"How long have you been here?"

Mac nodded.

"A couple of days. You've been in and out of consciousness, but I think the worst is over."

"Thank you."

She smiled. "It's what partners do for one another."

A repetitive voice rang in his ear. "Commander ... Commander are you still there?"

"Where was she when you last had contact?"

"Heading south. She's with guerrilla forces that don't have standard communication equipment. If we don't hear from her soon, we'll have to assume the worst." He paused. "Anyway, I thought you'd want to know. I'll keep you posted."

"Thanks." Mac returned the receiver to its cradle and glared at the pile of papers on his desk. He swung his good arm back and struck the stack. Papers went airborne then floated onto the floor.

Mac struck a wooden match and lit his pipe in a circular motion across the tobacco. He drew in a long mouthful of smoke and exhaled. A sweet aroma filled the room. He rocked back in his chair, reconstructed Atwater's phone conversion, and contemplated his return to the Far East.

A young clerk with a crewcut and dark horn-rimmed glasses entered his office. "The Captain wants to see you, Sir."

Mac ignored the request.

"Now, Sir."

Mac's face and neck reddened. "Get out."

The clerk turned on his heels and scurried away.

Mac stormed over to the Captain's office. His secretary, a middle-aged woman with a reputation of terrorizing the secretarial pool, tilted her head toward the door. A cigarette dangled from the corner of her mouth as she typed.

Before the Captain could say a word, Mac blurted out, "I need to go back to China, Ted." He plopped onto an overstuffed chair. "It's important."

Ted and Mac had been friends since their Academy days. He had been a groomsman at Mac's wedding. Although Ted outranked him, alone they omitted military formality.

"Mac, we need you here. Your work analyzing the German tactics is invaluable."

"Oh, come on. There are several guys who can do just as good of a job."

Ted remained quiet.

"This is punishment—punishment for screwing up my last assignment."

"No one is punishing you." Ted leaned back in his chair. "Now what's so important about China?"

"My partner's in trouble."

"I'm sure they have able men over there that can assist."

"No damn it. This is my responsibility. She needs me."

"She? Oh, I see."

"It's not like that." Mac rolled his eyes.

"So you need to play the hero."

"You're not listening. I owe her. She was—is—my partner." But he knew in his heart that there was an element of truth in what Ted said.

"It's late. Go home, Mac. Get some sleep. We'll talk again tomorrow."

MAC GRABBED HIS HAT AND OVERCOAT FROM the coatrack and walked outside. The early evening was pleasant with very little humidity. He threw his coat over his shoulder and muttered to himself. "Sleep, he says. Sleep isn't going to change anything."

He found himself at the tidal basin next to the newly constructed Jefferson monument. Across the way, the floral aroma from the last of the cherry blossoms filled his nostrils. It appeared surreal to him. This corner of the world was so peaceful with its brilliant colors and songbirds while elsewhere the grayness of death and suffering raged on.

Mac arrived home later that night. Helen met him at the door. "Where have you been? I've been sick with worry."

"I had some bad news and needed to clear my head." He removed his coat and threw it over a cream-colored, wing-backed chair then laid his hat on top.

"I'll heat your supper."

"Don't bother. I'm not hungry."

"You have to eat."

His stern stare caused her to turn and walk away. Always impeccably dressed, Helen cut a figure with her platinum blonde hair and violet eyes. She turned other men's heads, but his passion for her had waned. His desire was not for another woman but a more challenging existence.

Espionage is what I was trained to do. Why else would they send me to the Naval War College? This is not the right time for marriage. He sank back against the tuxedo couch, laced his fingers behind his head, and looked up at the ceiling. *I know what I've gotta do.*

TWELVE
Southwest China

THE DAY GREW HOT AS THEY MARCHED through the trampled bamboo. Mosquitos bit Anya's hands and face, but she refused to swat them away as punishment. She festered with anger and regret. She had been responsible for the farmer's death. *Those eyes—I'll never forget them. Was my life worth his?*

By late afternoon, the group stopped to rest in a grove of trees. Overhead monkeys peered at them as they picked pyramid-shaped vibrant green fruit. She watched them bite into the skin and peel away the rind and eat the flesh.

"What are they eating?" Anya said.

"Delicious delectables," Mei said. "The low hanging fruit is gone. You'll need to climb the tree if you want any."

Anya smiled. She recognized the challenge. She squatted, sprang up and snagged a limb. She wrapped her leg around it and pulled herself up. She shimmied higher until the branches were too weak to hold her. The monkeys leaped to other trees with disparaging screeches and whoops. She plucked a fruit the size of an orange. The skin was thick and bitter as she bit into it. She peeled it away to expose dark pink, almost red, flesh. Its patterned segments resembled grapefruit.

She took a bite. "It's sweet— refreshing." Juice dribbled from the sides of her mouth as she took another bite.

"Throw some—" Mei face lost all expression and she froze.

"What is it?" Anya's muscles tightened.

Loke motioned for her to stay while the others took to the jungle. Heavy footsteps marched toward her. She wrapped herself around the trunk and hid her white face. Her camouflage clothing and the thick foliage would help to conceal her.

Japanese voices grew louder. Five soldiers stood directly below her. A wintry shiver snaked through her. One soldier kicked the dirt in search of something. He knelt and touched the ground. He unholstered his pistol and scanned the area. Anya feared he would look up.

The other soldiers fanned out and searched the

perimeter. Anya held tight to the tree. A monkey jumped onto a nearby branch, which caused ripe fruit to break free. The thump on the ground caused a soldier to investigate. He picked one up, smelled it, and looked skyward. Anya remained motionless. Another soldier pulled him away before he could inspect closer.

The sun descended before Anya felt safe enough to climb down. She reached the last branch, but her foot slipped. She hit the ground with a thud and fell to her knees. Before she returned to her feet, the jungle leaves rattled.

"Mei, is that you?"

A Japanese soldier emerged with one hand on his gun, the other on a whistle that hung from a string wrapped around his neck. His lips neared the metal whistle. He stopped. His face turned ashen. He collapsed and fell forward. A knife handle protruded from the middle of his back. Several feet behind him stood Mei.

Anya thanked her with a nod. Loke and Jones dragged the dead man off the path, threw the corpse into a gulley, and covered it with debris. Mei followed the men. She returned with her knife back in its sheath.

Anya addressed the group. "They're sure to come back."

"We'll have a fighting chance if we get off this

path and make our way to the river," Loke said.

The four struggled along an overgrown animal path. Vines clung to their feet and low hanging branches swiped across their faces. Anya questioned why they were going up the mountain rather than to the valley and the river, but she kept it to herself. The relentless pace and heat took its toll on her. Out of breath, she had to rest.

"Shouldn't we be finding shelter?"

"We're almost there," Loke said. "Let's press on."

Not wanting to handicap the group, Anya put one heavy foot in front of the other. Every muscle screamed stop. A fog of conscious and unconscious thoughts ebbed and flowed as she trudged forward. It seemed she could no longer go on.

Loke spoke, "We're here."

"Where?" Anya said.

Loke pointed to what appeared to be an abandoned animal den. A dugout along the hillside was partially hidden by green vegetation. The opening was in the shape of a large mouth that looked to swallow a person whole.

"We can spend the night here. Anya, you and Lieutenant Jones crawl in and remain hidden. Mei and I will scout around for food and look for any signs of being followed."

Jones entered on his knees. Anya sucked in a

reluctant breath and followed. Pebbles stuck to her palms as she maneuvered inside. "I hope whoever owns this place doesn't come back."

The den dipped downward to create a hole, which gave them enough room to sit without clunking their heads on the cave ceiling. The two sat cross-legged and waited. Filtered light from the entrance cast a glimmer toward the end of the cave. Anya was surprised at the comfortable temperature. Her hands fidgeted in the awkward silence.

"Lieutenant?" Anya said.

"Kevin, please."

"Where are you from, Kevin?"

"The Big Apple." He went to tip a cap he no longer possessed. "That's New York, Manhattan to be exact."

"What did you do back home?"

"When we weren't carousing, Dodger games—that's baseball. I know I should love the Yankees, but those Dodgers, they're the best in the league. You just wait 'till next year. Leo will take 'em to the World Series. Only this time, we'll beat those damn Yankees."

"Did you attend college, or hold a job? Are you married?"

"Tried college. Didn't like it much. Had to study things that didn't interest me." He smiled. "I joined the Navy, went to flight school, did well, took some officer educational courses, and then they sent me to the war college—barely squeaked by. Fortunately, I was an ace piolet, so they stationed me outside Kunming with the Army Air Force bombing Japanese strongholds in Burma. Regrettably, one engine caught a shell and down we went. I can hardly wait to get back in that cockpit and bomb the hell out of them Nips."

"We?"

"We, the crew and I. I bailed out last and lost sight of them. Hopefully, they hightailed it to safety."

Anya heard a strain in his voice. "You said the War College? The one in Rhode Island?"

"Yeah."

"I have a friend who went to that school. Maybe you know him, Mac Benson?"

Jones tried to contain the roar of laughter as he slapped the side of his leg. "Pretty Boy. That's what we called him. All the ladies carried a torch for, ol' Mac boy."

Jones' mood had altered to a more relaxed state. Anya believed he was reminiscing.

"How's Mac doin'?"

"Home resting with his family, I suspect."

Jones brow furrowed.

"He was here in China—that is, we were here

together. He was injured and sent home last week. He was the one who suggested that I bring you home. However, I don't think he knew it would turn into a rescue mission."

"Yeah. Sorry about that. My parachute got tangled in the trees. I hung there for hours unable to cut myself loose when a Nip patrol came by." He scratched his chin growth. "I watched frozen, without a thought, as their guns pointed up at me. I thought for sure they were gonna use me for target practice. Instead, they shot at the cords, and I fell to the ground. I think they planned to exchange me for one of their own."

A noise outside caused them to freeze. A shadow blocked the light coming into the entrance. Anya feared it might be a bear returning to its cave. As the shadow neared, Anya made out the figure of a man. Friend or foe, she was not sure. She placed her hand on her pistol.

"It's me," Loke said. "Mei's behind."

Anya sighed and reclined. Backs against the wall, facing one another, they scrunched together in the cave. Mei handed out berries and more of the sweet green fruit that Anya enjoyed. Loke handed her a small solid object.

"What is it?"

"I brought back grasshopper, crickets, and bamboo worms—"

"Stop. I don't want to know." She closed her eyes and popped a solid object in her mouth. It had a crunchy, bitter lemony taste. *One is enough.*

"There's no sign the Japs are close on our trail, but I know they are searching for us," Loke said.

"What do we do?" Anya said. Mei remained quiet as they spoke to one another in English.

"I say we head for the river," Jones said. "We can make better time that way."

"He has a point," Anya said.

"It's faster but has a higher risk of being captured," Loke said.

"Maybe we should split up," Jones said.

Anya released a sarcastic snicker. "The only people who know this area are these two."

"Right," Jones said. "The men take the river. The women stay on the path."

"I don't like it." Anya now understood Mac's dilemma when Atwater ordered him home before he completed his mission to assassinate Chang Kai-shek's head of security, although later OSS aborted it.

I must insist that I stay with the lieutenant, no matter what he says.

THIRTEEN

ANYA STRETCHED HER LEGS AND YAWNED. THE cramped dirt cave's stale oxygen made her lightheaded. She stewed about the idea of splitting up the group. Her responsibility was to ensure that Jones returned home—alive. Before she could voice her opposition to Jones's suggestion, Loke cleared his throat.

"We need to stay together. Four guns are better than two."

"Okay," Jones conceded. "But our best chance is the river."

Anya and Loke nodded.

"We'll need to acquire a sampan," Loke said.

"A what?" Jones said.

"A boat." Loke's eyes shifted to Anya. "Mei and I will find a village and commandeer one."

Anya's stomach twisted at the image of coming

into contact with another villager. "Maybe we could steal one."

"The community would rather be shot for working against the enemy than as unwitting bystanders."

A fragment of light was all that remained as the sun set. Anya watched the last rays fade. At dawn, they would make their way to the river. The promise of everything not going smoothly weighed on her.

LOKE HAD RISEN BEFORE EVERYONE ELSE AND climbed a tree above the leafy canopy. He had spotted a village along the river. The four maneuvered down the hill slower than they would have liked. It had rained overnight and the path was muddy and slick as glass. Jones lost his footing on a small rock and fell taking Anya with him. They slid a few feet collecting a slurry of mud on their clothes.

"Christs sakes, Jones," Anya said.

"Sorry. It wasn't planned." He tried to get up but continued to slip and fall again.

A smile crossed Mei's lips as she helped him. Jones and Anya tried to remove clumps of mud, but it smeared even more.

"You can wash when we get to the river," Loke said.

They reached the edge of the village and hid amid the trees and tall shrubbery. Japanese soldiers with rifles slung over their shoulders milled around the town center. Villagers went about their duties, and children played as if the soldiers were invisible.

"Now what?" Jones said.

"They're probably searching for you," Loke said to Jones. "Mei and I will pretend to visit relatives. You two stay out of sight."

Loke and Mei handed over all their weapons except the knife Mei refused to relinquish. Anya and Kevin kept a close eye on Loke and Mei at a safe distance.

The two entered the town on a well-worn dirt path. The town housed several multi-story shanties with wide leafed ivy-covered rooftops. One house stood out with its red door. Different sized sampans lined up along the shore. A Japanese patrol boat moored next to them. In the middle of the river, a fisherman cast his net and reeled it in again and again. Each time it returned empty.

Loke and Mei made their way toward an elderly man who rested next to a sampan mending his net. Before they could reach him, two soldiers blocked their path. One raised his voice and pushed Loke to the ground with the butt of his rifle. Anya balled up her hands in fear that Mei would reach for her knife, but Mei remained steady. Loke lay in a fetal position. The soldier yelled and kicked him multiple times. Loke stayed fixed with his hands over his face and his arms protecting his sides. The soldier got in one last kick before he walked away. Loke twisted toward the trees and got on his feet.

Anya sighed. "He's okay."

Loke and Mei approached the old man. He sat and listened for some time and then stood, bowed, and meandered over to his boat. Mei climbed aboard the covered sampan followed by Loke and the fisherman who paddled them upstream.

"Let's make our way upriver to meet them." Anya slung two rifles over her shoulder, then she and Jones paralleled the water as fast as they could manage.

They joined the others who waited at the bank of the river. After they passed over their weapons, both Anya and Jones dove into the water to wash off the caked-on mud. They did not linger for fear of a patrol boat or worse—alligators.

The old man maneuvered his vessel through the current while his passengers sat in silence. Anya ached for the adventure to end and the pilot to return to his unit. *All I want is to find Joe and retrieve my ring.*

"What will you do after we have finished?" Anya said.

"Travel back through the bush and rejoin the guerillas," Loke said.

"You would be a valuable scout for U.S. troops."

"My need is greater with my people."

"Yes, of course." Anya admired Loke's dedication. "I will miss you and Mei. And you, Lieutenant Jones. What are your plans?"

"I will return to my unit." He leaned back and laced his fingers behind his head. "But first I want to take a hot shower and eat a giant, juicy steak."

The three chuckled. Mei smiled, not understanding what he had said. Their laughter was cut short at the sound of a motor. It approached from the rear. All heads turned to Loke.

"Patrol." Loke's body stiffened. "You—" He pointed to Anya and Jones. "Dive overboard and swim to shore. They witnessed us climb aboard back at the town. We'll pick you up after they pass."

Without thinking, Anya jumped and swam to the opposite shore from Jones. The bow of the patrol boat navigated around the bend. Anya hid in the brush in hope they would not investigate.

A pronounced voice from a megaphone commanded the boat to stand down for an inspection. The Japanese boat puttered and pivoted parallel alongside the sampan. The soldier's rifles bore down on them. Mei and Loke sat on a wooden bench where weapons lay hidden underneath. The fisherman stood braced against the long oar.

Anya retrieved the gun from her boot and released the firing-pin safety. She hoped it would still fire after being submerged. Lieutenant Jones was without a weapon. The patrol boat held four Japanese soldiers. Anya assumed the rest remained at the village and these were the unlucky ones ordered to investigate.

A monkey whooped above her. Heads turned her way. She ducked behind a tree. A shot echoed and the monkey dropped at her feet.

Anya's heartbeat echoed in her ears. Droplets of sweat formed on her upper lip. She crawled backward along the floor of the jungle and pushed back the pain from ants that bit her hands and face. The rustle of nearby leaves froze her cold.

FOURTEEN

A JAPANESE SOLDIER STOOD LESS THAN A YARD from Anya's face. Her finger pressed against the trigger of the .45. The soldier bent to pick up the monkey he had killed. She knew they considered monkey meat a delicacy, especially the brains. His head turned and he caught sight of Anya. She fired point-blank at the soldier's chest. Exploded, pieces of raw flesh flew out in all directions. A chunk splattered on her uniform. Gunpowder was thick in the air.

Another Japanese yelled out from across the river to his mate. A moment later, a multitude of gunshots rang out. Anya popped up above the brush. Loke struggled with a lone soldier. Anya could not see Mei or the fisherman. Jones struggled to climb aboard the sampan. She dove into the water and arrived on board to see Mei on the deck holding her stomach. Blood seeped between her fingers.

Anya rushed over and knelt beside her. "Oh, Mei, what have they done?"

Loke knifed the last soldier. He and Jones flung the body overboard.

"Where's the fisherman?' Jones said.

Loke said, "He was shot and fell overboard." The two men rushed over to Mei.

Anya remembered Sun's gunshot to the gut. She and Mac did not think he would survive, but he did. *After all, she's ten times tougher than Sun.* "She needs a doctor."

"Let's take their boat," Loke said. "It will be faster." He climbed aboard the patrol boat. Jones carefully lifted Mei and handed her to Loke.

Machine guns were riveted fore and aft on the 25-foot steel vessel. In the center were the controls, a wheel, and throttle along with several dials. The engine was still running. Jones unthreaded the boat from the sampan, and Loke jammed the throttle into high gear. They sped up the river looking for the next village in hopes it would be void of any patrols.

Mei panted as her head rested in Anya's lap. She looked up at Anya with glassy eyes. "Hold on, Mei," Anya gently squeezed Mei's hand. "We're almost there."

Mei lifted her arm to touch Anya's face. Anya held her hand. Mei smiled. Her grip went limp. She expelled a last gasp.

"Loke," Anya yelled. "Stop. Stop. Stop."

Loke slowed to a putter. Anya sat motionless. Tears streamed down her cheeks. Her head tilted up to see moisture fill the men's eyes.

Anger swelled inside Anya. "I am so sick of this war and all the dying." The culmination of all she had witnessed while on assignment was too much as she cradled Mei and wept.

Loke knelt beside her and touched her arm. "Mei was a good soldier and lived her life according to what she believed. We do not have the luxury of mourning her. But we will make sure that when we reach the next village, they will bestow the right of passage so she can make her way into the next life."

A MONASTERY EMBEDDED HIGH ON A ROCKY mountain peeked above white billowy clouds. Anya spotted hundreds of stars that ascend the mountain then disappeared in a shroud of mist. Had Buddha guided them there? Anya thought.

The stone village below appeared centuries old. A group of men sat on boulders, eating bowls of rice. They put down their chopsticks and watched Loke power the boat toward a sandy beach. The water was deep enough the engine did not wedge into the ground.

Loke jumped out and approached the men. An old man pointed his bony finger toward the monastery. Loke yelled at the others still aboard. "I need to retrieve a monk from his ivory tower."

"How long will that take?" Anya said.

Loke shrugged.

"What about the boat?" Anya said. "The enemy is probably not far behind."

"You'll have to sink her," Jones said.

Loke lowered his eyes, sighed, and approached them. "Take her out to the middle and plug her till she goes under. We'll be back in the jungle—and vulnerable."

"Sounds like we don't have a choice," Anya said.

Jones lifted Mei's body and handed it over to Loke. Anya threw their guns and ammo onto the shore. Loke pushed the bow of the boat offshore. Anya and Jones paddled to the middle of the river.

She straddled one of the machine guns, wrapped her finger around the trigger, and aimed it at the deck. Jones arranged himself in the same position. The two looked at each other, smiled and fired. Anya imagined the enemy as she let loose. The dhak-dhak-dhadak-dhadak sounded like a woodpecker drumming on a tree.

"That was exhilarating—almost cleansing," Anya said.

The vessel sunk within minutes.

Back on shore, Anya and Jones perched themselves below the roof rafters of the tallest building. Anya heard the patrol boat before she saw it. Over a dozen soldiers loaded on a boat slammed into the shore. All but one soldier disembarked and marched into town.

They shoved and pushed villagers around with their bayonets and demanded information about the American pilot. The crowd remained silent. A short, stocky officer shoved his rifle into a man's mouth. Women screamed and moaned. The officer blew a bullet through the man's skull. Anya jerked back and placed her hand over her heart.

Another man walked up to the officer. "We have not seen anyone by water or land."

The officer shot him. "Truth or you all die."

"They're going to rat us out to save their hides," Jones whispered.

A frail, hunchbacked woman hobbled over to the officer. "Two English traveled by and asked for food. We gave them rice and told them to leave. We do not want trouble. Please leave us in peace."

Anya recoiled at the prospect of another murder. Instead, the officer scanned the crowd and motioned for his soldiers to return to the boat.

"We owe them our lives with no way to repay them," Jones said.

"I don't think they do this for anything other than it's the right thing to do."

LOKE RETURNED HOURS LATER FOLLOWED BY A man dressed in a long reddish-brown robe with the tail of the fabric draped over one shoulder. The monk instructed several of the villagers to attend to Mei. They attempted to lift the body.

Anya intervened. "Where are they taking her?" She bit her upper lip and wrung her hands.

"It's all right. They are going to prepare her body," Loke said.

'What does that mean?"

"They will not go through the lengthy process of many days of prayer and mourning because she is not a villager, but they will treat her with respect and sensitivity. She will be wrapped in white cloth. There will be a short ceremony before she is cremated."

"How will that be done?"

"A bier will be built and her body placed on top. The flames will reduce her body to ashes, which will be scattered on the river so she can float to her new existence. A prayer will be spoken, something along the lines of …

> As rivers full of water
> fill the ocean full,
> even so, does what is given here
> benefit the dead."

Anya smiled. "I like that. Thank you." She watched the villagers carry Mei's body away. "God be with you, Mei." She had no more tears to shed.

Jones laid his hand on Anya's shoulder "We must press on—the Nips."

She patted his hand. "Yes. We need to get you home.

FIFTEEN

Anya swatted at flying insects and tried to avoid tripping over thick vines. She and the men had thanked the villagers and returned to the steamy jungle that smelled of damp earth mixed with a sour taste of rancid metal. The familiar animal noises of caws, whoops, and grunts, along with an occasional growl, were louder than usual. Light shimmered through the vast canopy of leaves as she surveyed the treetops. *Maybe they know something we don't.*

The Japanese had left the village and traveled north up the river. Loke suggested that they go east for several miles before they veered north to avoid an encounter. He used his machete to blaze a trail. Jones picked up the rear. Mei's death had affected Anya more than she had imagined. In her mind, she had lost a sister.

They were headed to Zuchi, an airfield occupied by Chinese forces. According to Loke, it would be two more days. The trek was taking more than a toll on her. She wiped the sweat from her brow and the back of the neck with a handkerchief. Her feet and arms became burdensome as if weights had been strapped on them. Her breathing became shallow. Her ears rang. Her head whirled. She took a step, then nothing.

Anya opened her eyes. Her whereabouts appeared murky, her thoughts disjointed. She was aware that Loke and Jones knelt beside her. Their drawn eyebrows caused her concern.

"What happened?"

"You fainted," Jones said.

"I've never done that in my life." She tried to sit up on her elbows, but everything spun around and she fell backward.

"Better stay put."

Loke gave her a sip of water from his canteen. "I think you're dehydrated."

"I'm sorry to slow things down."

"That's all right," Jones said. "I needed a rest."

Anya took another sip. The men helped her to her feet. "How much longer until we make camp?" She brushed dirt and leaves off herself and smoothed her hair with her fingers.

"We've made good time. We can rest here until tomorrow."

Anya believed Loke said that to make her feel she was not the cause. She sat on a rock while Jones constructed a campfire. Loke sliced open a vine and drained its water supply into a metal helmet. He poured rice the villagers had given them into the helmet and cooked it over the fire. The rice had a metallic taste, but she gobbled it up and felt energized.

Anya preferred the day's light, but the evening brought cool relief. However, with it came unseen creatures of the night.

Anya woke to muffled sounds. Loke and Jones were huddled together discussing something.

"What are you two up to?"

"Loke says we should start to head north for Zuchi."

"The sooner the better." Anya sat up and stretched. "That rice had something in it. I hallucinated that a tiger walked past me as I slept."

"That was no hallucination," Loke said. "A tiger checked us out as a possible meal."

"And you did nothing?"

"The bleating of the lamb merely arouses the tiger," Loke said.

"Old Chinese proverb?" Anya said.

Loke smiled. "We need to move out and gain as much time as we can before the mid-day heat."

Several hours had passed as they climbed a rugged hillside above the sticky heat. In the distance, the mountaintops retained winter's snowfall. A breeze circulated. Something Anya had not experienced since Chungking. The roar of a waterfall delivered the promise of a good soak. She stepped out of the jungle into a meadow. Water cascaded over skyscraper-sized boulders and emptied into a pristine powder blue river that took a lazy bend among the moss green landscape. Anya half-expected pixies to fly by in the picturesque fairyland.

It did not take long for all three to jump into the river, after removing only their shoes and weapons. Anya gasped a breath as the frigid temperature stung. Moments later, the refreshing liquid caressed her skin like velvet. She dove under and let the force of the water comb her hair. She popped up to see that Jones's face had turned ashen. Her head veered toward the shore. Several strange figures stood along the edge—crossbows drawn.

They were dark brown, barely four feet tall, but their features were fully developed. They had long black bangs and coarse straight hair that flowed past their shoulders. A piece of cloth draped from the right shoulder to the left armpit, leaving the left shoulder uncovered. Loke climbed out and spoke to them. Anya did not understand the dialect.

"These are the Qiu, an isolated tribe. They fear we will bring the Japs." Loke translated. "I've told them that they are our sworn enemy." The Qiu lowered their weapons. "They have invited us to a celebration. It seems they've killed a wild ox."

The Qiu's faces showed no sign of welcome. Jones faced Anya "They don't look too friendly."

Anya thought about the cannibals in the South Pacific who killed Captain Cook. The story was they ate him. She remembered what Mac had told her, "At some point, you must give into trust or you'll never survive."

Dripping wet, the three stuffed their boots on and picked up their weapons. They trailed the Qiu up the mountain to their village of two-story bamboo tree huts with long ladders that leaned against the tree trunks.

Anya was stunned at the tattooed faces of women and young girls. A teal green design of diamond shapes, lines, and dots at the brow ran down the nose across both cheeks to the chin. They wore black and white striped clothes made from a coarse sack material.

The villagers were very hospitable and treated them with kindness. A hunchback woman insisted on tattooing Anya's face. Not wanting to insult the woman, Anya acquiesced to a small tattoo on her upper arm. The woman rubbed a bamboo needle in a bowl of ink prepared from ashes. The woman pierced her skin with several short pricks. Anya winced each time the woman jabbed her. After she was done, Anya furrowed her brow at the indelible mark. "What is it?"

"A butterfly," Loke said. "It reflects good fortune in the Qiu culture."

At sundown, Loke spent time speaking with one of the old men as they sat around and shared a meal with the Qiu.

"What is he saying?" Anya said.

"He's explaining the ceremony that brought us this meal. They fasten an ox to a sacrificial pole. Women place a woven carpet onto its back and hang colorful beads on its horns. Everybody dances around it. They elect a young man of virtue to kill the ox. In a single blow with an ax, he decapitates the animal. Everyone cheers and the women prepare the ox for roasting."

Anya finished chewing and swallowed her mouthful of meat. Her thoughts reflected about their situation. She thought about the tiger proverb and wondered if they had poked the Japanese one too many times. She hoped they would not end up like the ox.

SIXTEEN

ANYA TURNED ONTO HER SIDE AND LET OUT A groan. Her upper arm was sore and swollen from the imprint of the butterfly tattoo. She questioned her decision to mar her body. *It seemed like a good idea at the time.* It had oozed during the night and formed a crusty layer. She lathered on a gooey salve the tattoo artist gave her. She had been told it would peel like sunburned skin in a few days to reveal the design.

Loke and Jones sat with the tribesmen and waited while the women prepared the morning meal of a rice-based pottage with vegetables. The men ate first, by tradition. Kevin gave Anya a sheepish look as he ate. Only after they were finished did the women and children eat.

After breakfast, two older men sat and played a board game using black and white round tiles while the fathers played with their children. Even though the Qiu's culture appeared strongly patriarchal, which irritated Anya, she admired their close-knit relationships and unfettered lives.

Loke approached Anya and Jones. "The Qiu told me they spotted a Jap patrol in the area a few days ago. It can't be the same soldiers we saw yesterday—they were going upriver." He rubbed his hairless chin. "They could be hunting game. But I fear they may have half their army scouting for us. We'll need to take extra precautions and avoid major trails and rivers."

Anya scanned the villagers. "We should give the Qiu a gift of thanks, but I don't have anything of value."

"They don't expect payment," Loke said.

"What about one of our rifles?"

"They wouldn't take it. For them, it's a matter of practicality. Once the bullets are gone, the tool is no longer of value. They prefer their crossbows—arrows are easier to replicate."

"Maybe we should ask for a crossbow," Anya said half-laughingly.

The men of the village escorted them to an overgrown animal trail. The three blazed their way along the mountain on their way toward the airfield.

The heat of the jungle replaced the coolness of

the village. The prospect of boarding a plane and flying out, leaving behind biting-stinging-sucking bugs, gave Anya renewed strength.

Hours later, the forest cleared to reveal a small dirt airstrip. Tall puce-brown weeds bordered it, with a few stragglers that popped their heads up between cracks in the runway. At the far end of the field rested a weathered wooden shack.

"It looks deserted," Anya said. "Shouldn't Chinese soldiers be defending it?"

Loke's brow furrowed. "Yeah, this doesn't feel right."

"Where's the plane?" Jones said.

The three spread out in different directions and scouted the perimeter. Jones found some boot prints and old cigarette butts but no sign of any troops or equipment.

"Maybe they're no longer using this field," Anya said. Her words had scarcely rolled off her lips when the jungle came alive with the sounds of crunching brittle leaves, crackling brush parting, and popping gun chambers. Nine Japanese soldiers in camouflaged uniforms emerged. The door to the shack flung open and five more charged out with Tommy guns aimed at them.

Anya's back stiffened. Her first instinct was to shoot. Instead, she followed Loke's lead and dropped her rifle. Jones held a firm grip on his.

"Put it down, Lieutenant," Loke said.

"I'd rather they kill me than become a prisoner."

"Please put it down, Kevin," Anya said.

"If you shoot, you kill us all," Loke said.

Anya gulped. "I don't want to die and have my body rot in this jungle."

A Japanese officer shouted at Jones. Anya glanced over at her companion with a pleading look in her eye. He hesitated then dropped his rifle.

Soldiers corralled them with their bayonets. Loke and Jones received the most pokes and prods. A heavyset soldier placed the tip of his blade against Anya's cheek. Her stomach twisted. Jones tried to protect her and received a blow to his gut and doubled over. The soldiers marched them to a truck hidden amongst the trees.

Loke and Jones boarded the back of the truck. Jones held out his hand to Anya and helped her up. A hand grabbed her bottom and pushed her forward. She knew not to make a fuss as it could easily escalate into something worse. She positioned herself between Loke and Jones. The soldiers piled in next. They squashed next to one another on benches the length of the truck. A stale odor of sweat mixed with exhaust lingered. A pang reverberated through her body. She teetered on whether her nerves were the source or a bad suspension.

The truck ambled along a potholed road. Anya worried over what lay ahead—torture—rape—

An aircraft overhead interrupted her thoughts. The roar of its engine grew louder followed by a high-pitched whistle. The truck careened to a halt, everyone piled out and darted for cover.

Anya headed for cover. She barely had time to crouch when a bomb exploded. Debris flew in several directions. Clumps of dirt pelted her back and hands that covered her head. Anya popped up to see the truck engulfed in flames.

"We're lucky," Jones said, "he probably had one bomb left in the bay. If I had to guess, I'd say, a small incendiary bomb. Not massive but it did the trick."

"How does it feel being the target, not the agent?"

"Up there," he pointed, "I'm a soldier doing my job. That's what a pilot thinks. I can't fault him for it. But it does give you a different perspective when you're the one on the ground."

Anya thought she read a flicker of remorse in his eyes. "Maybe someone came across the mayhem at the airfield and radioed ahead."

Soldiers dashed about with one exception—the guy with his gun pointed at their backs.

Anya looked around. "Have you seen Loke?"

"He was over—" Jones nodded to his left but

no one was there.

"He's gone," Anya whispered. "I think he escaped."

"That's why they're scurrying like mice in a field as if a hawk were flying overhead," Jones said.

Anya hoped he would return with reinforcements and rescue them. *But where were they being taken? How would he find them? Would he be in time?* She thought about what Loke had said, "Prisoners are a hindrance. Better to shoot them."

SEVENTEEN

SANDWICHED BETWEEN JAPANESE SOLDIERS, Anya and Jones marched along a rutty dirt road with rope bound around their wrists. Out in the open, away from the jungle canopy, the midday sun began to drain their energy. Anya bent her mind to yesterday's swim. The river's therapeutic water had flowed over her skin like a satin sheet. It had brought contentment she had not experienced since starting the journey to China. A soldier's loud voice broke Anya's meditation and transported her from serenity to misery.

She rubbed the tattoo on her upper arm and sighed. "My butterfly hasn't brought much luck."

The same heavyset soldier with a pockmarked face turned and pushed her with the butt of his rifle. He screamed at her in Japanese. "*Shaberanai.*"

Anya thought about whether to acknowledge

him, revealing that she understood him or play dumb. She decided on the latter. She held her gaze on him too long, and he jammed his rifle into her gut. The blow caused her to double over and cough. Jones squatted to assist but was yanked upright. Anya managed to stand on her own, although not fully straight.

"You be bad, get beat—beat very bad. You be good, you be happy," a soldier said in English.

Anya imagined grabbing the rifle from the swine and blasting a hole through his belly.

They marched until she thought the soles of her sore feet would disintegrate. The clouds rolled in and hid the sun giving Anya's cracked lips, sunburned nose, and burning cheeks a bit of relief. She looked over at Jones. He walked with his eyes closed. She wondered if he was asleep. She bumped into him. He opened one eye part way and glanced over at her with a half-smile.

Walking in their sleep must be something the military drills into them.

She thought she could no longer stand on her feet when the soldiers stopped and relaxed under the trees. They left Anya and Jones in the open. She crumpled to the ground along with Jones.

"These guys," Jones nodded toward the soldiers, "they're the group that was out on patrol when you rescued me."

"That heavyset bully has it in for us."

Anya observed how the bully resembled a monkey with protruding ears, pronounced forehead with eyebrows in the shape of devil horns. "He enjoys inflicting pain. I'll bet if he walked stooped over his knuckles would drag on the ground."

Jones leaned over and whispered. "I think I can distract them long enough for you to escape."

The thought of a getaway rejuvenated Anya's spirit. "What about you?"

"Well, you'll have to rescue me again." He winked.

She pulled her knees to her chest. "I'm afraid of what they might do to you if I escape."

"You must try for both our sakes."

Anya nodded.

While some of the guards lay with their eyes closed, others tossed around a small ball using their feet. Jones jumped up and raced toward the trees. Anya dashed in the opposite direction. A high-pitched scream froze her in her tracks. A rifle was on her before her foot had a chance to place the third step. She turned to see the heavyset soldier standing over Jones's unconscious body. He slapped a dense stick against his palm and smiled at her.

Is he dead? Her thoughts hardly left her when

Jones's arm slowly reached to touch the back of his head. *Thank God.* She was uncertain if it was gladness for him or the fear of being on her own with Japanese soldiers.

The heavyset soldier grabbed Jones by the back of his shirt and hauled him to his feet. He placed his fingers on one of Jones's eye-sockets and forced his eye open, then pointed to the sun. Jones squinted and looked away. The soldier walloped the back of his legs with the stick. Again, the soldier opened Jones's eye and pointed to the sun. If he moved, he hit him. If he looked away, he hit him. He hit him even if he blinked.

Jones stared at the sun. His fingers tore at the sides of his pant legs as tears flowed down his cheeks. His legs shook. His knees buckled and he collapsed. The heavyset soldier walked away as the others hooted and applauded.

Anya rushed to his side to console him.

"I can't see," he muttered.

She rubbed his back. "Keep your eyes closed and if you have a mind to, pray it's temporary."

The soldiers rose. They were off again. Anya helped Jones to his feet and placed his bound hands on her arm. "I'll guide you."

Twilight had descended by the time they reached a clearing. An abandoned farmhouse alongside a weathered thatched-roofed stable sat in the center of the deforested area. Anya thought it looked like the owner had taken any livestock they might have had, burned their fields, and headed north for safety.

A slender soldier led Anya and Jones inside the stable and stood guard at the doorway. Anya guided Jones to the far side of a stall and sat him on a pile of hay. "How are your eyes?"

"Still blurry and my head is pounding."

Anya knelt and examined his dark amber eyes. The whites were now red and his pupils were constricted to tiny dots. "Lay and rest. I felt a cool breeze from the south earlier. It smelled salty. I suspect we are near the ocean."

"You're probably right. The Imperial Navy has the Chinese coast locked up, so U.S. supplies have to run through The Hump."

"The what?"

"It's a hair-raising route over the southern Himalayans. I've never flown it, but I've heard stories. The aircraft are basically metal cans with wings. The pilots face bad weather with hundred-mile winds and clouds that obscure mountain peaks. There were so many wrecked planes over one stretch, the pilots dubbed it aluminum alley."

Anya gave Jones a half-smile. "I wonder what they plan to do with us." She paused. "Why haven't they killed us or worse?" she swallowed hard.

"I can't figure it," he said. "Maybe a prisoner swap. Whatever, it doesn't make sense."

Jones's face went pale. "I just thought of another reason—my godfather."

"Who's your godfather?"

"Bill Donovan."

"William Donovan, head of the OSS?"

"Yeah, you know him?"

"No, but do you think that these soldiers might know of the connection."

"That was my thought. But I'm not sure if that knowledge would help or hinder our situation. Let's not admit anything at this point."

"Right."

The guard sauntered over with a bowl, placed it on the ground, and returned to his post. A bit hesitant, Anya got up to retrieve the half-empty bowl of white rice. She passed the bowl to Jones before taking a bite. His shaking hand accepted it.

"Eat up. Who knows if we'll ever get another meal."

Finished, they both leaned back against stacked hay and sat in silence. Anya thought about what Loke had said earlier—you don't keep prisoners when you're in the jungle. *Why are we still alive? Where are they taking us?*

A scuffle was heard outside. Someone was

yelling at the guard.

"What's going on?" Jones said.

"From the shouts, our guards in trouble for his generosity in giving us some of his rice. A soldier beat him for it." Anya picked up their empty bowl and hid it in the hay. "Let's keep him on our side."

The heavyset soldier entered the stable and stared at the two with his hands on his hips. They both diverted their eyes to avoid a thrashing. He turned on his heels and left in a huff.

"At least he didn't make us throw up the rice," Jones said. "You have the strangest look on your face. What are you thinking?"

"My mother. She was about my age when she was murdered."

"If they were going to kill us, they would have already done so."

They sat in the dark using hay to insulate them from the brisk night air. The warmth relaxed the ache in Anya's leg muscles. To block out the stench of animal urine that filled her nostrils, Anya forced her thoughts back to when, as a young girl, she attended lavish parties at the tsar's palaces.

They sat in the dark using hay to insulate them from the brisk night air. The warmth relaxed the ache in Anya's leg muscles. To block out the stench of animal urine that filled her nostrils, Anya forced her thoughts back to when she was a young girl.

Her mother would tell her tales of lavish parties at the Tsar's palace with the promise that one day she too would attend.

A procession of sleds and carriages transported guests. Bejeweled women in colorful stylish gowns with narrow bodices and long flared-out skirts flirted with tall handsome men in red uniforms as their sabers and spurs clanked on the marble floor. The lavish hall was lit up with so many candles one would not know it was evening. Newly released butterflies flittered around the room and landed on spectacular artwork by such artists as Rembrandt, Rubens, and van Dyck. Meals were presented in a formal sit-down fashion with several courses consisting of soups, quail with truffles, pheasant with pistachio nuts, bass with ham, tortoise meat, and roast lamb. Guests sipped on red and white wines, beers, and vodka. After mealtime, an orchestra played beloved compositions from Korsakov, Bach, and Strauss. Men and women waltzed with elegant grace across the candlelit ballroom.

Her first dance would be with a handsome soldier. She imaged his soft brown eyes and cupid lips. But then the room went dark. The man's face morphed into a demon-like creature with black snake eyes. A deep scar ran across his face—it was Sun Temujin. He pinned her to the ground, ripped the red diamond ring from her finger, and tore at her gown. She struggled to free herself but his weight was too much.

Anya screamed and sat up wide-awake.

EIGHTEEN

LIEUTENANT JONES SHOOK ANYA. "WAKE UP."

Perspiration saturated the nape of Anya's neck and moisture filled her eyes. She gasped for breath. "I'm okay. It's ... just a bad dream." She pulled herself up, leaned against a bale of hay, and tried to clear her mind. She rubbed her naked ring finger, something she had not done in some time. *I need my talisman.*

"Do you want to talk?"

She shook her head. "I want to forget."

The cracks between the barn slats failed to reveal daylight and a hoot from an owl confirmed that the next day had yet to dawn. Anya turned to Jones. "Lieutenant, what did you do before the war?"

He chuckled. "My father referred to me as a lazy no-account bum."

"I might dispute that."

Jones raised an eyebrow. "If you knew me then—well—you might think differently."

"Tell me about your home so I can forget where we are for a moment."

He laced his fingers behind his head and drew a quirky smile. "Manhattan in a word is—magnificent. It's like a flower in full bloom. The tall buildings are its petals that stretch toward the sky. The streets are crowded with people, honking trucks, cars, and buses. Vendors on every corner sell everything from newspapers to franks and lemonade. They are the fertilizer for the city. Its fragrance is like no other. A bouquet of gas fumes, horse manure, and fish guts—a giant pile of hot garbage. It's the most wondrous place in the world."

"You love it very much."

"I loved the life I led, but those days are gone forever." His smile faded.

"What do you mean?"

"To jump in a cab and run uptown to jazz clubs. You know you're in for something special when a doorman dressed in a cap and double-breasted uniform greets you. The door opens and you realize that you've entered another world. Candles glowing from small table lamps resting on white linen. Women dressed in finery with candy apple red lips and men in black or white tuxedos.

The champagne never stopped flowing. I miss sipping brandy and the aroma of a smoked-filled room from a good Havana."

Anya envied the gleam in his eyes as he reminisced about his home. She had no one and no place to call home. An ache in her chest thumped.

A commotion from outside interrupted their conversation. "Where do you think they are taking us?" Anya said.

"We know they have thousands of forces working independently in the area. I think this lot has been cut off from their unit, short on supplies, and trying to find their way back, but I'm not sure if they even know what direction they're going."

"Why are we still alive?"

He shrugged. "Something tortuous."

"Like what?"

"I've been contemplating that. It must be either a prisoner exchange or a labor camp."

Anya shuttered at her possible destiny. In their minds, there was only one thing a woman was good for.

Their heads veered toward the door with the sudden appearance of the guard. He motioned for them to come. They walked outside as the sun inched its way above the horizon. A refreshing breeze swept past. PL, as Anya referred to the patrol leader, led the way as they lined up in a single file. They followed the soldiers who macheted their way through the jungle with their guard close behind. The narrow footpath held overgrown branches that scraped their faces attracting biting insects to their blood. She considered leaving a trail for someone to follow, but the immense wasteland grew so fast it seemed pointless. She was grateful for one thing. Monsoon season was weeks away. Otherwise, they would be ankle-deep in mud. The terrain had transformed into a mountainous obstacle course of dense bamboo thickets and underbrush of vines, briers, and razor-sharp grass as tall as a man. As the day wore on, the baking heat began to affect Jones. Although his eyesight had returned, he had not regained his fortitude.

Hunger unremittingly gnawed at their bellies. Some of the soldiers ate orange-colored berries as they walked. Because they were at the back of the line, it was easy for them to sneak berries and stalks of grass to eat. Their guard followed suit.

By mid-day, Anya considered faking a twisted ankle to force PL to rest. Her plan was set, but the soldiers had picked up the pace. *Why are they in such a hurry?* She reached the top of the hill to discover a godsend below—a pool of water. Several soldiers undressed and jumped in. Anya reached the water's edge. Some of the men taunted her to join them. Insolence prodded her to strip off her boots and dive in. One of the men swam toward her, but PL flagged him off. He ordered the guard to remove her from the water. He struck an authoritative pose with his hands on his hips as if to warn her not to do it again. She gave him a slight bow and rested beside Jones. The swim had removed the grit from her hair and clothes and revitalized her although the blisters on her feet still hurt.

"I'd like to get a drink of water, but I can't get my legs to cooperate," Jones said.

Anya rose from her squatted position without thought to her safety and walked toward the trees. The guard bared his rifle and pointed it in her direction. PL placed his hand on the barrel and lowered it. They watched as she pulled bamboo leaves from the tree and then walked over to the muddy pond and filled the leaves with water.

"Cup your hands."

Jones complied.

The water slowly filtered through the leaves into his hands. "It's jungle survival tactic that I learned from Mei. The leaves purify it to help prevent dysentery." Over her shoulder, she observed others follow her example. She spied PL who had joined in.

A few hours later, back on the trail, the sky had turned hazy and the smell of smoke loomed. The smoke grew more intense as they entered a clearing. Ahead were the remains of a bombed village. The once erect wood buildings now burned to the ground, still smoldered. An odor of rotting flesh soaked the air with a rank sickening sweetness like cheap perfume. Wild dogs, pigs, and raptors fed on bloated bodies that littered the area. The soldiers tried to shoot a boar, but a single missed shot scattered them back into the jungle. The troops rummaged around, but there was nothing left to pilfer.

If they had given me a rifle, I could have put a meal on the table. But they probably wouldn't have let me eat any of it—the filthy marauders. Anya's stomach pinched from hunger.

Across the way, the bully spoke in a low voice. A group huddled around him. The men's grumblings alarmed her as they looked her way. *What would happen if they were to consider Jones and me excess baggage? How disciplined are these men to follow this leader?* She knew well enough that hunger and fear could break down command and create mutiny. The men's angry voices grew louder.

NINETEEN

DISGRUNTLED TROOPS ADVANCED TOWARD PL. A single shot rang out. Anya's heart pounded as she froze. Her eyes darted in the direction of the incident. A Japanese soldier dropped to the ground. Blood flowed from his chest. Smoke lingered from the discharge of PL's gun. Unfortunately for Anya and Jones, it was a faceless follower rather than their nemesis.

After the flare-up, the bully seemed to keep his distance. Jones had commented that it seemed as if a black cloud had lifted, but Anya kept vigilant.

They were back along the trail when the column halted. PL motioned to their guard. A soldier jammed the butt of his rifle into Jones's ribcage and motioned him to his knees. Anya complied at the sound of rumbling in the distance. The rest of the troops hunkered down in the brush.

The noise increased to a clap of thunder and the ground vibrated. Past the thicket, Anya saw a caravan of Chinese trucks. A few infantrymen sat on tanks as they motored past. She considered screaming, but it would have been pointless. She wondered why PL did not try to disrupt the motorcade. He was outnumbered and outmanned, but that had not deterred other Japanese troops from impeding the enemy. She had read foreign correspondence reports that the Japanese were experts in jungle warfare. They were known to perch themselves in trees and shoot troops as they passed or hide among a small group of villagers wearing a cone-shaped straw hat then drop their tools and pull out an automatic weapon.

Maybe Jones is right. PL is on some kind of mission.

THE SUN WAS ABOUT TO SET WHEN THE TRAIL ended, exposing a village. Unlike the last one, this one was intact. There was a scarcity of villagers, a few old men and women, and a handful of children. Anya wondered where the others were. The rice fields seemed too large for this small group to manage. *Maybe the others have gone off to fight.*

A villager, who wore a gray queue that touched the ground, confronted PL. He gripped his machete as the man's high-pitched voice screeched.

PL stepped back but the villager pressed on with his raised cane. The blow was so swift Anya's mind went blank as to how it happened. The man's knees buckled before his head separated from his body. Villagers wailed. Anya clutched her belly and bent over. She straightened up after her nausea subsided. PL stood with a stoic expression.

What message is he trying to send to his men?

Within moments, the troops went on a rampage. They stormed throughout the homes like a crazed pack of wolves that hadn't eaten in weeks. They smashed anything in their way and stomped those who got between them and what they wanted, even their own men. The villagers huddled together. Anya and Jones stood silent for fear any distraction might draw their attention and possible retribution. Even their guard appeared bewildered.

Amidst the chaos, the guard led them to a small windowless room and locked them in. Anya felt safe for the first time since their capture. She believed he was acting in their best interest but skeptical as to why.

She removed her boots and massaged her sore feet. In the darkness, she heard women and children scream. She remembered when the Kempeitai secret service had arrested her in Shanghai. She had been caged next to a young girl. She knew what that child's outcome would be—the same as outside her door. She covered her ears to quell the cries.

"He's permitting them to let off steam so he can better control them," Jones said.

"What?"

"The commander knows there's dissension, but if he can give them what they want now, he can gain their allegiance tomorrow."

"Why must they act like wild dogs?"

"Rape and pillage have been going on since before the crusades. Besides, this might be to our benefit."

"Well, I don't have to like it."

"It's not for the civilized, but what enlightened society goes to war?" He tried to place his arm around her, but she pulled away.

ANYA AWOKE TO THE RATTLE OF THE LOOSE door handle and a creak as the door opened. The bully emerged, gripped her by the arm, and pulled her out without allowing her to put on her boots. The brilliance of the day caused her to squint. It took several moments before she could make out objects. She winced as sharp rocks pricked the bottom of her feet. He dragged her across the square to a tall narrow building. The walls inside were covered from ceiling to floor with dark wood. In the center was a lush courtyard garden with well-pruned plants in decorated pots that flourished from the sunlight overhead. Several elaborately carved sliding doors led to various chambers on either side.

The guard pointed to one of the rooms. Anya was certain that she was being given up as an offering. She crept through the doorway to find a soldier laying on a bed shivering. Next to him was a washbasin. An old village woman, whose gray bun was wrapped as tight as the lack of empathy on her face, dipped a rag into a bowl of water, squeezed it out, then wiped his brow. Anya felt his skin. It was hot to the touch. She knew in an instant that he had contracted malaria.

PL stood over the man and pointed to him. Anya shrugged. He grabbed her head and planted her face a breath away from the man. She struggled to free herself unwilling to help the dying man. He yelled at the bully to retrieve Jones then released his grip. Water dripping off the cloth into the washbasin broke the silence.

The bully returned with Jones and placed the barrel of the gun at Jones's temple. Anya believed she had no recourse but to reveal that she spoke Japanese. "I can't cure malaria. I can prevent the possibility of getting it by rubbing certain leaves on exposed skin."

PL stepped back, startled. "If you can

prevent—you can cure. If he dies so does your friend. A life for a life."

Anya thought for a moment then ordered the village woman to gather leaves and bark from a specific tree, the one with white flowers and large dark green leaves. The woman returned. Anya asked her to fill the bucket with water and boil them. *If it can prevent insect bites, maybe a soup might cure it.* She hoped this would save the soldier and, consequently, Jones.

After two days of feeding soup to the ill man, his fever broke and he regained his senses. Anya was relieved but undecided if the soup or his constitution got him through it.

BACK IN THE CUBBYHOLE WITH JONES, ANYA heard footsteps. She hoped helping the soldier might improve their treatment. "Hopefully they are bringing us food."

The guard prodded and pushed them outside as dawn was about to break. He marched them back into the narrow building. Anya knew by the tenor in his voice that something was wrong. They entered the invalid soldier's room. She gathered from his ashen gray skin that he was dead. PL pointed his gun at Jones.

TWENTY

ANYA RAISED HER VOICE AT PL. "WHAT happened?"

"You killed him." PL pointed at the dead soldier lying in bed.

Her brow narrowed which caused her forehead to wrinkle. "Impossible. He was fine a few hours ago."

PL backslapped Anya hard enough it almost knocked her off her feet. "Well, he's dead now."

She threw back the covers and saw the victim lying in a pool of blood. "This man didn't die of malaria. He was castrated." She rubbed the sting from her cheek. "His death was not my doing."

PL stormed outside. The guard herded her and Jones to the center of the village. The soldiers rounded up the villagers in front of PL. He hollered at them in Japanese for several minutes then motioned for one of his men to interpret.

"Who disgraced one of my men?"

Anya knew why he had been mutilated. But now the entire village was at risk. PL walked up and down the line between each villager with his questions. They remained quiet. At various times, he slapped a few across the face with a switch. His face graduated to a dark red and his jaw clenched. He walked away from the group. With his back to them, he nodded to one of his men who pulled his pistol from its holster and fired. A child fell to the ground. It remained undetermined if he meant to kill the child, or they happened to be his first line of sight.

That was monstrous. Has the jungle turned them into animals or have they always been that way?

Someone in the crowd yelled out, "It was the old woman."

PL searched the group but she was gone. "Find her."

"She's there," a young boy the Little Resisters' age pointed to the river. The troops forced everyone to the river.

Facedown in the water with arms stretched out like a crucifix, the woman's body bobbed in a sea of red, her gray bun still intact.

A village elder spoke. "We killed her for her act in hopes that you would spare our lives."

PL demanded that all the villagers get into the water, next to the body. A shiver passed through Anya. She knew what was next. She prayed his honor would prevail.

"Wait." She marched up to PL and pulled him aside. "Are you sure you want to do this?" She could barely swallow, her throat was so dry. "These are innocent people. Is not the death of the old woman enough?" The soldiers remained stationary as their eyes darted from PL to Anya and back.

"I am not a barbarian, but I must do my duty as an officer."

"Your soldiers raped women and children. You killed an innocent child. Do you need an entire village's blood on your hands?"

"I must show strength—to maintain respect."

"Would it not be more heroic, more admirable, more courageous to walk away?"

PL glared at her. Anya's eyes remained fixed on him. He turned and walked up the embankment. She breathed a sigh of relief convinced he had retracted his order. She followed him but stopped when she heard gunfire and spun around to see soldiers fire into the crowd. Bits of skull bone and dismembered limbs blew into the air. Mangled dead bodies floated in the water. Anya's stomach twisted. She ejected what little matter she had.

THE NEXT DAY THEY WERE ON THE TRAIL AGAIN. The soldiers had bundled up the villager's food, killed any chickens they could catch, and left the place ablaze. Anya thought she saw movement in the brush as though eyes were watching them as they left. She could not stop thinking about the atrocity these soldiers had perpetrated on innocent people.

I hope there is a hell because these people need to burn for their crimes.

They reached a murky river to find the anchorage of a bridge was all that remained. Frustrated, one of the soldiers shot off a round into the trees where a colony of bats hung upside down. The bats shrieked, dropped their guano, and filled the sky drowning out the sun as they swirled. Anya looked at Jones and rolled her eyes. She glared at PL who turned away.

PL ordered Anya and Jones to enter the putrid water. Jones led the way. She knew they were being offered as bait. She silently beseeched the river gods to let the alligators, crocodiles, adders, and pythons sleep. The water level was waist high on Anya. She managed to keep her balance between the slippery river rocks and the current. However, at one point she lost her footing and sank up to her neck. The river water refreshed her after the march in the hot sun.

Almost to the other side, Anya froze at the chilling screams that echoed from behind. She turned to see a fourteen-foot gator wrap itself around the last soldier's body. It slapped the water as it twisted and rolled. Everyone raced toward the shore. Anya's heart pounded so hard she thought it would explode. She scrambled over Jones to get out of the water. He helped her maneuver the high riverbank. Too exhausted to run, they fell, panting to catch their breaths. Anya faced Jones. "Three dead nine to go. At this rate, we may be the only ones to survive." They both snickered.

"What you laugh at?" The bully jabbed the butt of his rifle into Jones's ribs.

Jones winced, "Just happy to be alive."

He raised his rifle over his head to strike, but PL grabbed his arm. A look was all it took to set the bully back in order.

PL did not take the time to mourn their comrade before they started back on the march. The path had altered from a narrow overgrown jungle trail to a well-worn rugged mountain road. PL drove them until the sun set. There was no shelter so they lay alongside the road. As the blood-red sun sank behind the mountains, Anya fell asleep.

A LOUD EXPLOSION WOKE ANYA. SHE SAT UP AND said to Jones. "What was that?"

"Bombs"

"Ours or theirs?"

He shrugged.

Dawn was breaking when Anya noticed there were fewer soldiers. "Where do you think they've gone?"

"Probably on reconnaissance."

The men returned hours later and huddled next to PL. They whispered their findings.

"It must be the Chinese convoy that passed us the other day, otherwise they would be making a beeline back there," Jones said. "Our guys are so close. I think we should make a dash for it."

"That plan didn't work too well last time."

"I know, but I think we must try."

She thought about how men, especially young men, seem to reveal in defying death. She remembered Mac also had a daredevil attitude. She considered the alternative, swallowed hard, and nodded.

TWENTY-ONE

JONES PREPARED TO MAKE HIS MOVE TO ESCAPE.

"Wait," Anya whispered.

"Why?"

"The scrub is not high enough to use for cover. They'll be able to pick us off easily. We can't outrace bullets. Let's wait until dark."

"We might be miles away by then, and the Chinese unit may have moved on."

The bray from an unseen animal ahead gained everyone's attention. PL motioned to his troops. They dropped to one knee and drew their weapons. Anya held a faint breath and waited for the animal to round the bend. Meat for dinner, she thought.

Jones said, "Let's go while they are distracted."

Anya nodded. She took a step but something caused her to pause and turn. She glanced at the road ahead. Voices echoed—young voices. Jones tried to pull her away, but she refused to budge. A withered old mule with its head hung low stumbled into view followed by a tall, thin, silver blond man holding the reins. Three Chinese children's faces peered wide-eyed through the front rib of a once, canvas-covered wagon. Two girls appeared to be preschool age while the older boy looked around seven. To see the faintest smiles dawn over their sad suffering little features rendered Anya incapable of leaving.

"I can't go," she said. "There are children at stake. You go." She tugged on his sleeve. "Don't forget to come back for me."

Jones nodded then made his escape.

The tall, thin man halted the mule. PL yelled for his men to hold fire. There was a momentary stare-down. PL turned to Anya. He motioned her to his side. The two approached the wagon. The tall man's face was sun-weathered and his clothes—almost rags—hung off his skeletal body.

PL asked Anya to translate.

She addressed him in English. "Who are you, and what are you doing here?"

"I am a missionary seeking a safe harbor for these orphaned children. We mean you no harm."

Anya recognized the man's Australian accent.

"Have you seen any enemy patrols?"

The man shook his head.

"Do you have any weapons?"

"I am a missionary, not a soldier."

"Please answer the question."

"No."

PL ordered one of his men to search the wagon. The children cried. The missionary pulled them out of the wagon and set them on the ground. His gentle manner and soft voice seemed to calm them.

Anya approached the oldest child. His bug-bitten face looked as though he had contracted the pox. She spoke to him in Mandarin. "What is your name?"

"My Christian name is Jacob."

Anya's eyes grew wide. She flashed back to what Mac had said about crossing paths with some missionaries and a boy named Jacob. "Do you remember an American named Mac?"

The boy nodded.

Anya looked over at the tall, thin man and spoke to him in Mandarin. "You must be Mathew."

"Yes—"

Anya interrupted him. "Don't acknowledge you know what I'm saying."

The man remained stoic without expression.

PL interrupted them. "You speak Chinese?"

"Mandarin," she replied.

"What are you saying?"

"I asked the boy his name."

"A very long conversation for a name."

"I also asked where he was from."

PL grunted at her. He ordered his men to stand down when nothing of value was found in the wagon. The snap of rifle and gun hammers recoiling gave Anya a sense of relief. She looked around for Jones—he was gone.

She was glad he had escaped. He would bring back troops to rescue all of them. PL realized Jones was missing and ordered two men to go after him, but not before he backhanded the guard.

Anya sat on the ground and rested beside Mathew with Jacob on her lap. PL watched them. She sensed he was contemplating what to do with the new arrivals.

"Mathew, you don't look well," Anya said.

"I hear the angels calling, my dear." He patted her hand. His touch felt cold.

"What brought you down this road?"

"Though we are in the hands of the enemy, I believe God led us to you."

Anya chuckled. "I think you got lost."

"A walk of faith can never be by sight."

Anya studied his solace face. This gangly, easy-mannered man had a reverence about him that she believed could convert even the most faithless.

"Mac said you had a wife."

"She died several weeks ago. Her fever boiled her brain. We lost several of the children as well. God rest their souls."

"I'm so sorry." She nestled the children that sat beside her.

"The bitterness of death shall pass, and I will take my place in heaven."

Anya feared that if he closed his eyes he would never awaken. She resumed her conversation. "Where did you come from?"

"We have been traveling for weeks looking for safety, but every town that discovered we were missionaries spat on us and chased us off. We have suffered greatly from the power of the sun and lack of sustenance. The little ones sob uncontrollably due to raw blisters on their arms from shoulder to wrist, because of the burning blaze of the sun. I plucked leaves from trees by way of covering their open sores, but it is little comfort."

Jacob's short pants exposed his scarred legs. Anya rubbed them as if to wash away the pain.

The guard set a bowl of rice and a canteen of water in front of them. Anya looked over at PL and gave him a slight bow. She thought she observed a glint of sadness in his eyes before he turned away.

The children circled, dipped their fingers into the bowl, and scooped out a few grains of rice making sure to leave enough for the others. Anya lifted the bowl to Mathew who refused to partake.

"Let the children have their fill," he said. "I possess a bitter shame for my inability to help these poor wee souls."

"You must eat."

"Tomorrow." His voice faded. He laid his head on the ground and closed his eyes.

The scouting party returned before dark. Anya overheard them say that they had killed Lieutenant Jones as he ran.

Those bastards shot him in the back.

She placed one hand on her mouth to avoid making a sound and be accused of eavesdropping. The other hand grabbed her churning stomach.

The children ... I must not upset them.

She clenched her jaw, curled her fingers into fists, and restrained her tears. She would remember Lieutenant Jones with a fondness. Her focus now was to survive—more for the sake of the children than herself.

TWENTY-TWO
Washington D.C.

MORE THAN A WEEK HAD PASSED AND MAC HAD yet to hear from Atwater. Ted had convinced him that Anya would turn up before he reached China, so he agreed to remain in Washington—for now.

Mac carried on with his daily mundane tasks, but his thoughts were never far from Anya. He poured through various German newspapers and magazines to glean insights that might alert the U.S. government of impending issues. His efforts did not go unobserved. He had rendered an important discovery that caught the eye of the president. A reporter in Hamburg had inadvertently referred to an old dynamite factory. The finding had been relayed to the British who ascertained it was a functional manufacturing facility and bombed it.

The ring of his phone pulled Mac away from his studies. He reached for the receiver in hopeful anticipation. "Commander Benson."

"Ted, here."

"Oh, it's you."

"Is that any way to speak to your superior?" He chuckled.

"I thought you might be—never mind."

"Can you come to my office? I'll have my secretary bring in lunch. I like to discuss something with you."

Ted was a topnotch guy in Mac's eyes, a straight shooter who told you how it was and never abused his rank. Mac thought of him as the kind of leader who knew how to bend the rules to satisfy everyone.

Mac took the last bite of his ham and mustard sandwich and washed it down with a swig of Pepsi. "Okay, what's up?"

"American command in London has a need for someone with your skills. It's temporary, a couple of months at the most."

Mac rubbed his chin and pursed his lips. "If you recall, that didn't work out so good a few years back." He remembered the time he had infiltrated German intelligence in London. When his cover had been exposed, he had been forced to kill a

German spy—a woman.

"New season, new mission."

"You know I have an issue at home," Mac said.

"I can work that avenue."

Mac raised one eyebrow. "Good luck with that."

"I know you've been itching to get back into the field, and this may be a path."

"Let me get back to you." Mac went for the door.

"Stop by for a snort before you leave tonight."

Mac gave Ted a mock salute and walked back to his office. *This assignment could be a way to show that I am ready to get back out there.* He heard his phone ring and raced into the office. "Commander Benson."

It was Atwater. "Bad news, Mac. We received a report that Anya and her assignment have been taken prisoner."

Mac sank into his seat. "When?"

"We received word from someone who was with her but escaped. The report is over a week old. They're on the march through the jungle. Intelligence says it's been hard to pick up their trail."

"I'll catch the first flight out."

"I'm not sure you can do anything that isn't already being done."

"I need to be there."

"Understood. I'll make arrangements with your commanding officer."

"YOU DON'T UNDERSTAND, HELEN." MAC PACED the room of their flat. You don't leave a fallen soldier in the field."

Helen jammed her hands on her hips. "Are you in love with this woman?"

"It's not like that. She was my partner. I owe her my life twice over."

"What about me? What about your daughter? We need you."

"It's not about need. It's about doing the right thing—loyalty."

"Your loyalty should be to your family. I can't live like this—your coming and going on a whim."

"You might remember in between your coffee klatches and pinochle, there is a war going on."

Helen stomped her foot. "I volunteer at the canteen and sell war bonds. I have my service flag in the window." Her bottom lip trembled. "I don't want to have to change that blue star to gold."

Mac stopped pacing. "You knew when we married where my first loyalty lay. If this were any other time." He hesitated. "We all must sacrifice for a cause greater than ourselves." He raked his fingers through his hair. "I can't be the man you think I am—I have my orders. I've made arrangements with Ted. He'll check in on you from time to time."

"If you leave again," she pointed a finger in his face, "we won't be here when you get back."

"That's up to you, but I have to go." Mac headed for the stairs.

"Where are you going?" she said.

"Upstairs to kiss my daughter and pack."

TWENTY-THREE
Southwest China

THE SUN ROSE ON ANOTHER DAY AS THE soldiers readied themselves to march. Anya overheard PL tell his men he wanted to get an early start having lost time yesterday. She nudged Mathew to wake up, but he remained motionless. She touched his bare arm to roust him. His skin was as cold as snow.

Mathew was right after all. Death had crept in and stolen him away.

Anya approached PL. "The missionary has died. I would like permission to bury him."

"No." His gaze refused to meet hers. "We must push on."

She stared unflinchingly and persisted. "These are Christian children who have been through a harrowing ordeal. It's important they see him buried."

"No."

"But—"

"You are trying my good nature. If you persist, I'll have you all shot." He spun around on his heels and walked away.

She huddled the children and explained to them that Mathew had gone to heaven. The girls cried. Jacob looked up at her and folded his hand around hers.

"It will be all right, Miss."

Tears welled up and rolled down her cheeks. "Let us pray."

They held hands next to the body and bowed their heads. Anya had not prayed since she was a young girl. Words failed her. Instead, she listened to the children recite the Lord's Prayer. PL allowed them to finish before he headed the troops out.

Anya removed all the flea-infested hay. The ride would be less comfortable for them, but they would be better for it. She loaded the children into the back of the wagon, climbed onto the wagon seat, and took hold of the reins. The old mule hobbled along too weak to last more than a day. Their guard walked alongside. It unsettled her to leave Mathew's body lying open on the ground, but she hoped it might alert someone to their location.

Anya heard a commotion and looked over her shoulder. Two soldiers lifted the body and flung it over the side of the steep ravine.

Damn. They think of everything.

She glanced down to see that the children had nestled themselves as close to her as they could manage. Their dark almond-shaped eyes turned up to the heavens were filled with holy dread.

The mule plodded along. The wagon's wheels managed to hit every rut. After several hours of riding in the wagon, Anya's back ached. *I'm not sure what is worse—walking with blisters or riding in this torturous vehicle.* She opted to walk. She gripped the mule's headstall to ensure he advanced.

"Jacob, do you know any songs?"

"Yes, Miss. We know the Jesus song."

"Can you all sing it for me?"

Their frail voices eked out a few stanzas.

> "Jesus loves the little children
> All the children of the world."

Anya smiled remembering a similar Russian song as a child.

> "Red and yellow, black and white
> They are all precious in His sight
> Jesus loves the little children of the world."

Their voices grew louder as they continued until PL silenced them with a stern glance. He turned around, and Anya stuck her tongue out at his back. The children laughed. Giggles still rang in her ears when PL's head swung around. They marched on and on with nothing to break the silence but the footfall of the old mule.

Anya realized the children had not cried or shown any sign of fear since Mathew's passing. *The normal thing would be for them to cower and cry. Had they become impervious to their condition? Do they believe that this is now a normal part of their lives?*

She was taking more risks confronting the enemy. She thought about their situation. *Now that Lieutenant Jones has reportedly been shot, why are we still marching? Maybe PL is not the boss. Maybe he's waiting for instructions from another.*

Anya turned her attention to their guard. He no longer held his rifle ready to fire. Instead, he slung it over his shoulder. He walked in a stooped manner as though a heavy weight pulled him down. The rest of the unit, even the bully, lumbered along. Not PL. He stood upward and marched with vigor. *Maybe some of these men are as weary of this trek as I. Where in the hell is he taking us?*

IT HAD NOT BEEN MORE THAN A FEW MILES when the old mule stumbled and fell. He snorted a final breath before expiring. The mule was too sickened to be considered food.

"Well, that's the end of the ride. We'll all have to walk." Anya helped all the children out of the wagon. She hoisted the littlest one on her hip. The children's rags barely covered them, and they had no shoes but they seemed past noticing it. Her tattered clothes hung looser these days.

Anya plodded along carrying one child with two others tagging behind. She led them like a benevolent pied piper. She admired their resiliency, their faith, their bravery. She was unsure if she could have endured such a journey at their age.

But what choice does any of us have?

They had left behind the dry brush terrain and traveled into trees that reached to the heavens. PL deviated from the road and took everyone along a narrow trail. A half hour later, they found themselves beside a stagnant pool. Clouds had hidden the sun most of the day, but the heat still lingered. While the soldiers swam, Anya gathered leaves and filtered the water. It had been more than twenty-four hours since she last had something to drink. She sat at the edge of the bank with the children as they dipped their aching feet in the refreshing water. Mindful not to let the children, especially the girls, venture too near the soldiers, she kept them close. After what had occurred at the last village, she knew these men's appetites.

The eldest girl, about five, picked some wildflowers and presented them to Anya. She stared at the purple and yellow arrangement, then plucked a few from the bouquet and placed them in her and the other girls' hair. The girls covered their mouths and giggled. Jacob asked to share in wearing a few flowers. It lifted her heart to see them savor a bit of joy in their awful circumstances. PL watched them. Anya imagined he was pining for his own family. After their fun, they ate the flowers.

PL had them back on the road within the hour. They marched and marched and marched. Anya repositioned the child she had placed on her hip piggyback style to relieve the ache in her hip. She was about to ask PL to stop and rest when a shot rang out.

A bullet caught one of the soldiers in the neck. He dropped to the ground without knowing what hit him. The wildlife fled, monkeys howled and leaped from tree to tree while the birds took flight. Everyone scattered off the road. Anya hustled the children and sought shelter among the bushes. The soldiers blindly fired back.

God, I pray it's the Chinese army.

TWENTY-FOUR

ANYA KNEW THE DIRECTION OF THE SHOT. IT came from in front of them. Since a blaze of fire did not follow, she assumed it was a lone shooter. She wondered if it could be a Chinese soldier or perhaps one of the Little Resisters. PL motioned for two of his men to go around and flush out the sniper. The two encircled the target, leaving five to defend themselves and their guard to watch over her and the children.

Anya wrapped her arms around the children and nestled them close to her like an eagle protecting her eaglets. The girls' shivers vibrated against her body. Jacob tensed his muscles with his fists ready to protect. *He's such a brave little guy.*

She watched as the soldiers' heads bobbed up and down and sideways about the brush trying to draw out their enemy. One man snaked along the ground inching forward. PL motioned for two more to circle round. The surrounding area went silent. The gunfire had ceased as quickly as it came.

A shout emanated from the brush. "He's gone, Sir."

"Did you see him?"

"No, Sir."

"Everyone back on the road and stay focused," PL said.

Anya waited until all the soldiers were on the road before she brought the children out from their hiding place. PL marched at the head of the line. The soldiers' heads jerked in anticipation of another ambush. Anxiety filled Anya wondering if the sniper was after the Japanese or all of them. She decided to keep a good distance from the soldiers—as far as their guard would allow.

Before sunset, PL stopped the unit for the night. The heat had subsided replaced by a nip in the breeze. Anya and the children huddled together. Their mumbled prayers reverberated in the still of the dusk.

Anya and the children woke to hysteria. A soldier addressed PL. "We have lost another during the night, Sir."

Anya noticed his short pant legs quiver as his bare knees knock together. She searched around and spotted a soldier's face in the dirt. He appeared as though he were sleeping. She crept closer and saw a well-defined slice in his back shirt where a knife had penetrated.

"Where was the night guard?" PL said.

The soldier bowed his head. "He fell asleep, Sir."

"If we weren't short of men, I'd have him shot."

Anya wished PL would carry out his inclination. The night guard was the bully. He had been getting aggressive toward her lately, walking past and shoving her aside. One time, she caught him pointing his gun at her. His monkey face with those devil-horned eyebrows danced up and down as he laughed exposing missing teeth.

Anya readied the children for the day's march. Before PL ordered everyone to move out, he motioned her to his side. "You and the children will march in front."

She knew he was using them as a human shield. Even their guard was upfront with them. Fear filled his eyes. She lined up the children behind her. PL yelled at her to stop. He had the soldiers place the children alongside her. She wanted to reason with him but knew it was futile. *He cares no more for them than the dirt that clings to the bottom of his shoes.*

Jacob piped up. "It's all right, Miss. God is with us."

"I hope so," she mumbled. They all held hands and dawdled along until PL shouted at them to pick it up.

Yesterday the soldiers stumbled along and lugged their guns. Today they were alert with rifles prone to fire at will. Several had multiple weapons confiscated from fallen comrades.

Anya noted the return of the noisy monkey howls and bird screeches. This gave her a sense of calm that all was right—for now.

The sweetness from a light rainfall moistened the air. The damp roadway twisted and turned as they ascended to a ridge. The soldiers behind them made it seem to Anya as though she and the children were on their own. But the occasional snort, retched discharge followed by a splat in the dirt brought her back to reality.

The smallest child squeezed Anya's hand. Anya knew that the little ones were tired. She refused to continue. PL yelled at her.

"The children are tired and need to rest."

"You march."

Disgusted, Anya squatted and motioned for the littlest child to climb on her back. Without instruction, their guard slung his gun over his shoulder and picked up the other small child. PL remained silent. Anya believed PL would rather they proceed than belie their guard's act of kindness.

When they reached the top of the hill, PL ordered everyone to rest. The tired and thirsty children slurped up muddy puddles of rainwater. The soldiers drank from canteens they had filled at the last pool. Their guard poured some of his water into the hands of the child that he had carried. Anya smiled and gave him a nod of thanks. He shared some of his water with her as well as the others.

He pulled out a tattered black and white photo and handed it to Anya. The picture was an image of a woman sitting with a child on her lap. A man stood beside them.

"Is this you?"

He nodded.

"Your wife and son?"

He nodded again.

She returned the photo with a better understanding of why he aided the children. He carefully returned it to a leather wallet and tucked it into his jacket pocket next to his heart.

The children had lain down to nap. Anya leaned back against a boulder and closed her eyes. She flashed back on how she had gotten to this place in her life. How her boss at the War Department had assigned her to assist Mac in

Shanghai and how she wound up in Chungking with Joe.

Joe. I wonder if he has found Sun? I've got to get these children to safety and retrieve my ring.

A shot rang out. Anya's eyes popped open. Her mind consumed with sixes and sevens as the children scampered next to her.

A soldier lay dead in the dirt. Another got up and darted into a grove of trees. A bullet caught him in the back before he cleared the roadway. His arms stretched out, and his back arched before he fell.

Too dangerous to run for cover, they lay as flat as possible on the ground. Anya had no visual contact with PL but heard him shouting orders.

"He's hiding in the trees. Aim high and kill that son-of-a-bitch."

A barrage of Tommy gunfire was so loud it forced Anya to cover her ears. The children cowered their heads with trembling arms for protection. The bombardment continued for what seemed an eternity.

"Cease fire. Cease fire, damn it," PL said.

The explosion gave way to an eerie stillness.

"Go find him."

Anya looked up. Where tall trees once stood, their tops had vanished. Several branches dangled, clinging to trunks. The air reeked of gunpowder.

She wondered how many creatures they had slaughtered in their attempt to kill one man. She calculated how many soldiers remained. *Five.* She felt confident that she and the children were not targets. The sniper could have easily picked them off.

The three soldiers who had gone out to investigate returned. "Nothing, Sir."

"What?"

"Sir, we found nothing."

"Impossible."

"There were dead birds and monkeys and debris everywhere but no human, Sir."

"We have got to take a stand and kill this *baka* before there's no one left."

TWENTY-FIVE

BEFORE PL'S ASSAULT PLAN COMMENCED, ANYA moved the children behind a large boulder. She nestled close to them with her arms wrapped around their little bodies, ready to take a bullet if necessary. Her greater fear was not from the sniper, but the possibility that the soldiers might turn their anger toward them.

Two soldiers ran into the forest with guns ablaze. PL crouched behind the scrub about ten feet away. She watched him reload his pistol and fire blindly. The bully knelt on the other side of PL.

A shot rang out. A soldier yelled, "The sergeant's dead."

Moments later a second shot discharged.

PL shouted, "Private, where are you?"

No response.

"Private?"

No response.

Only three remained, and Anya knew it. She looked at PL. His brow furrowed, and the corners of his mouth drooped. Capitulation gripped his face.

A loud crack rang out. Its echo resounded in the silence.

PL sat on the back of his legs with glazed eyes. His head slumped forward into his chest. Anya crawled next to him and felt for his pulse. She laid him on his back. PL looked up at her and smiled, then his head rolled to one side. Even though he had been her captor, she felt he had always kept her safe from his troops. He was gone. She knew the inevitable.

The bully came after her like a hungry bear without thought of the sniper. "There's no one to save you now, you white whore. You and those children are dead meat."

Anya drew on instinct rather than conscious thought. She picked up PL's gun. She fired again and again and again. The bully's eyes rolled back into his head as his bullet-ridden body staggered forward. She repeatedly pulled the trigger even though the chamber was empty. He stopped a foot from her and collapsed. Shaking, she dropped the gun and looked around for the children. They ran over sobbing, seeking comfort.

"You're safe." She patted their backs. "We're

all okay now." She searched for their guard but found no trace. *He must have fled.* She wished him well for his acts of kindness to her and the children.

Anya searched PL's pockets looking for a map. Something, anything, that could tell her their location or nearest village. She pulled out a small notebook from his inside jacket pocket. She thumbed through the pages. It read like a diary with all the details of their march. But it did not tell her where they were going or why she and Jones had been taken prisoner.

She pulled the compass button from her jacket. *Thank God for Army ingenuity. We'll simply head north. Maybe we will run into a village that can help us.*

A rustle from the bushes caused Anya and the children to freeze. She held her breath as a figure emerged. "You're a boy," she exhaled.

He held his arms above his head. His right hand gripped a rifle. A loose-fitting tunic and pants hung off his thin frame with a satchel slung across his body. He looked the same age as one of the Little Resisters.

Anya rose to her feet. The children clung to her. All except Jacob. He held a wide grin on his face as he looked up at her. "He is our savior, Miss."

"Indeed, he is."

"My name is Bo." He lowered his arms. "I will

take you to a village where they can help you."

"Thank you, Bo."

They followed him along a narrow trail. The overgrown weeds along the sides towered above the children's heads.

Freedom makes the air smell renewed. Like a stiff breeze has blown out the stench of captivity. Her thoughts rolled to the future. *Once the children are safe, I will find Joe. Once I find Joe, we will find my ring.*

The farther they walked, the calmer the children became. At one point, they launched into a song about hiking.

Anya caught up to Bo several yards ahead. "How did you locate us?"

"I was away from my village hunting for monkey meat." He paused. "I returned to discover that my people had been slaughtered. It was easy to follow the marauder's trail. They have no understanding of how to cover their tracks."

"The one soldier —you let him live?"

"He aided the children. No man who holds kindness toward children would willingly massacre innocent people. But if he is a bad person, the jungle will consume him soon enough."

"What will you do now?"

"Fight to regain my country."

A profound sadness swept over Anya at the loss of his childhood. "Hopefully the war will end soon and we can go back to living."

"We can never go back. War changes everything. No one is untorn."

"Yes, indeed." She was reminded of her father putting her mother and her on a ship to Shanghai before he set off to join the White Russian Army only to die a year later from Lenin's assassin—Sun.

Jacob ran up to Anya. "Miss, the little ones are thirsty. Me too."

"How much farther, Bo?"

He pointed ahead. "When the sun reaches the ground."

She calculated the sun's downward trajectory on how long it would take to reach the horizon. "Too many hours away," she said. "We need to rest and find food."

"This path follows the water." Bo veered off the trail through the bush. A few yards ahead lay a creek. After a healthy drink, the children romped in the water to cool down. Bo pulled some dried fish meat from his satchel and handed a share to everyone. Anya tugged at the hard-boiled meat with her teeth. The chewy substance had a bland taste. Nevertheless, she was grateful for nourishment.

The short break was over and they returned to the trail. The rest by the water had refreshed them, however, the heat took its toll in only a matter of hours. Exhausted, Anya carried the littlest one.

Jacob tried to help but the others were almost his size.

It seemed they could walk no farther when the jungle opened to a village nestled between several mountains. Wooden buildings with upturned eaves on roof corners dotted the hillside. The surrounding area was green and lush. Rice fields covered every surface of flat ground. It reminded her of the scene in Hilton's novel, *Lost Horizon,* when the half-frozen travelers entered Shangri-La.

Anya walked to the center square. A multi-tiered red tower with green eaves stood out as a meeting place. Unlike previous villages they had encountered, this was a prosperous one. The people had full faces with clear skin and bright eyes. Some were on the verge of being chubby. They dressed in freshly laundered clothes, not tattered as she had witnessed in other villages. Wide-eyed women huddled together. Some covered their hands over their mouths and whispered. Anya was not sure if they were afraid or curious. The men stood and stared.

Bo approached an elder with a long white wispy beard wearing a black cap and a floor length purple gown. The distance between them made it difficult for Anya to hear their conversation. A child tugged at her and she turned away. When she looked back, Bo had vanished.

TWENTY-SIX

FIVE DAYS AFTER MAC LEFT WASHINGTON, HE landed in Kunming, China, through the Himalayas, a white-knuckle flight he believed would be his demise. His legs wobbled as he deplaned. He released a sigh when his feet touched solid ground. *Give me the open sea to turbulent air travel.*

The pilot slapped Mac on the back. "Any landing you can walk away from is a triumph."

Mac rendered a half-smile as the pilot walked into the makeshift terminal. A tall young man dressed in brown khakis approached him with a salute. "Commander Benson, I'm Sergeant Walters. We received notice you were coming."

Mac returned the salute.

"If you will follow me, Sir, Colonel Colson would like to speak with you."

The sergeant wheeled the jeep around the

dusty roads and through the center of town. The city streets were swollen with Chinese who had fled inland years earlier to avoid Japanese bombs. Vacant eyes and malnourished bodies showed him the desperation these people faced on a daily basis.

The jeep entered the Army compound after submitting to scrutiny at the guard shack. Walters stopped in front of a two-story wooden building. The sergeant remained in his seat as Mac jumped out.

"The Colonel's waiting inside, Sir." Walters gave Mac an intense look. "Find her, Sir."

"What?"

"Miss Anya. Find her, Sir." Walters drove off before Mac could respond.

Mac walked through double doors into an expansive entryway. Behind the reception desk sat a clerk, barely old enough to have enlisted. The clerk paused his two-finger typing and looked up. "Can I help you?"

"'Commander Benson. I'm here to see Colonel Colson."

The chair hit the floor with a bang as the clerk jumped out of his seat with a salute. "Sorry, Sir."

Mac did not take it personally given he was dressed as a civilian. Command had asked him to wear his uniform. He packed it instead.

"Top of the stairs. First door to your left, Sir."

The clerk held his salute until Mac reciprocated.

Mac reached the top of the stairs. He peered around the corner. A clean-shaven, gray-haired man sat at his desk shuffling through papers. Mac interrupted him with a knock on the door.

"Come in. Come in. You must be Commander Benson." Colson rose from his seat, walked around his desk, and offered his hand rather than a salute.

Mac started to salute but abandoned it to accept Colson's hand.

"We've heard a lot about you, Commander."

Mac furrowed his brow. *Had Ted or perhaps Atwater been talking?*

"Please have a seat." Colson sat behind his desk. "Command gave us the skinny on why you've risked your life to come here."

Mac nodded. "Do you have any info on a possible position?"

"It's tricky over here. There's a lot of places to hide—jungles, caves, and tunnels—but I believe there is someone who can assist you."

Mac heard footsteps and swung around. He was stunned for a moment then his mouth flew open. "Jonzy, you son-of-a-bitch. It's good to see you." The two shook hands with a tight grip. Mac slapped Lieutenant Kevin Jones hard on the back.

"Our girl's in trouble, Mac."

"That's why I'm here."

Colson said, "You boys probably want to get on the road. I've got a jeep waiting out front packed with supplies."

"Thanks, Colonel." Mac shook his hand and he and Jones headed outside.

Mac turned to Jones who sat in the driver's seat. "Where are we off to?"

"To pick up our guide."

TWENTY-SEVEN

ANYA SETTLED INTO THE VILLAGE'S LIFESTYLE. She decided not to leave the children immediately due to their failed health. She thought they would acclimatize themselves after a few days, and she would be on her way. But a day became days and then a week. She struggled to find the right time.

A villager provided her and the children with a modest house where they could sleep and prepare meals. Others supplied clothing and shoes for the children. She shed her camouflage uniform for a patterned sarong that wrapped around her waist and a long-sleeved white blouse rolled up to the elbows. One farmer gave her vegetables, another rice. A woman showed her how to pluck a dead chicken by putting it in hot water for a few minutes, pulling out the feathers and squeezing out any stubborn pinfeathers. She thought to gut a fish stunk but, a chicken—that was enough to make her forgo meat.

Evenings, before bed, were everyone's favorite time. They huddled together on the bed as Anya related fairy tales she remembered from childhood. Their favorite was the one about the boy who inherited a wise cat that wore a hat and boots. Anya lowered her voice, at a climactic point as danger approached, her voice grew louder and louder and then roared. The girls jumped and giggled but not Jacob. He thought they were silly. The girls especially loved that in the end, the hero married a beautiful princess and they lived happily ever after. Jacob would crinkle his nose, he preferred the cat.

ANYA WAS ON HER WAY TO THE WATER WELL when she overheard whispers. A cluster of elders discussed their distress over the strange white woman who had invaded their peaceful village.

"You must forgive them. They have never seen an Occidental," said the old man with the wispy beard.

She pulled the filled bucket from the well and emptied the water into her pail. "You can tell them I will be gone soon."

"They know, yet remain fearful. They are stuck in tradition and cannot see the good in something different."

"I have lived within many different cultures, and I'm familiar with being on the receiving end of that fear." Anya lifted the pail ready to leave then set it down and turned to the sage. "Why did you agree to take us in?"

"It is our custom, most of us that is, to help those in need. Treacherous times call for extraordinary strength and compassion."

Anya was unaware her teeth were embedded in her lower lip until she sensed pain.

"Worry shrouds your face."

"I'm concerned about the children. What will happen to them?"

"What do you want to happen?"

"I hope to leave them in the care of your village."

"They will be safe here amongst their own. The boy," he paused, "he is fond of you—maybe too much."

Anya nodded. "I've tried to get him to play with the others, but he insists on staying by my side. He believes I require protection."

"Convince him to attend school with the other boys."

"I'll do my best."

ANYA STRADDLED A LARGE ROCK AT THE EDGE of the river and used it as a scrub board to wash clothes. Jacob stood in the river. He rinsed, wrung out each piece, and then laid them on the rocks to dry.

"Jacob, what do you want to do when you're older?"

He turned to her. "Fight to free my country like Bo."

She stopped scrubbing to push strands of hair back in place. "What if the war is over before you have a chance? Then what?"

He stopped what he was doing to contemplate. "I think I'd like to be a preacher or a doctor."

"Those are admirable but lofty goals. To accomplish either one will require an education."

He furrowed his brow. "I guess."

"You've attended school before, right?"

He nodded.

"Did you enjoy it?"

"Yeah."

"They have a school here." She stopped to stretch her back. "Maybe you could inquire tomorrow."

Jacob shrugged. "Maybe."

Anya lowered her head and smiled.

THE NEXT MORNING JACOB TROTTED OFF TO school without a fuss. Anya wished to follow to see how things went but knew better. She wrestled with her thoughts throughout the day on how to approach him. How could she tell Jacob that she had to leave? The girls were already smitten with a childless couple that agreed to take them in.

Anya waited anxiously for Jacob's return. When he did, he barely got through the front door before she quized him.

"How was school?"

"Okay."

"What did you learn?"

"Stuff."

"Did you make friends with anyone?"

"Some."

Anya sighed. "Jacob, I want to hear about your day."

Jacob kicked at the floor with the toe of his shoe. "The teacher chalked arithmetic on the board, and when I knew all the answers, she left. Another teacher came in and I was moved to a new class. After lessons, we took a break and played for a while then back for more lessons and I came home."

"Did you enjoy it?"

"I guess."

Anya sat on the settee. "Jacob, come sit next to me." She patted the seat. "I need to tell you something." Jacob sat beside her. She placed her hand on his shoulder. "It's important that you fit in here and do well. Do you understand?"

He nodded.

Anya twisted her lips and took a breath. "I must leave—"

"Where are you going?"

"I need to return to my home."

"I want to go with you." Tears welled up and spilled onto his cheeks.

Anya tightened her arm around him. "You need to be brave and be a big brother to the girls. I have found a very nice couple who are willing to have all of you live with them."

Jacob nestled his head on Anya and sniffled. "I'll be brave—promise."

Loud voices filtered in from outside. The noise cut Anya's hug short. She rose from her seat and opened the front door. The voices progressed to a disturbing volume. Alarmed, she and Jacob walked toward the center of the village. People had formed a circle around three strangers near the community building. They were dressed in camouflage uniforms with rifles slung over their shoulders. They appeared familiar to her. One turned her way. She slapped a hand over her opened mouth and then removed her hand exposing a wide grin.

TWENTY-EIGHT

ONLOOKERS CHATTERED, POINTED, AND TRAILED the foreigners who had entered their village. The elder with a wispy beard approached them and spoke in broken English. "You look for Miss Anya?"

The tallest man nodded.

The old man pointed a bony finger at Anya several meters away.

The man studied her. She was barefoot, wearing a white blouse and blue sarong wrapped about her waist. Her sun-kissed skin glowed a shimmery brown like mink. Her Titian red hair was gathered in a tangled mess atop her head. He waited for her to acknowledge him.

Anya shaded her eyes with her hand and stared with puzzlement at the tall stranger. Jacob was the first to recognize one of them. "Mister Mac. Mister Mac." He ran and jumped onto Mac almost knocking him over. Mac had no choice but to catch and lift him. Anya's knees almost buckled. She pushed back loose strands of hair, straightened her sarong, and walked over. Mac put Jacob down. The boy refused to relinquish his claim and clung to his leg.

"I thought I'd find you surrounded by enemy soldiers," Mac said. "Instead, you've gone native."

Anya wrinkled her nose at him and smiled. "How's the arm? The last time I saw you, you were recovering from a bullet hole."

"Shipshape and Bristol-fashion." Mac rotated his arm.

"How on earth did you find me?"

"It wasn't easy, but I had lots of help."

Anya raised an eyebrow in question. The movement to Mac's right caught her attention. She gasped, "Oh—my—God." Tears flowed at the sight of Kevin Jones. "I thought they shot you."

"Oh, they tried," Kevin said. "I tripped and rolled down a ravine. I bounced off a few rocks before I landed at the bottom." He rubbed his ribs. "It was steep enough that it would be hard-pressed for them to climb down. They let off a few shots, but I was protected by a rock shelf."

Anya wrapped her arms tight around Kevin's chest and hugged him. He groaned. She released her grip and wiped moisture from her cheeks. "I'm not sure I can stop crying. Why aren't you flying bombers?"

"I haven't checked in with my squad." Kevin placed a finger to his lips. "I had unfinished business."

Still wiping her face, she said, "It's so wonderful that you are both here."

"Someone else is here too," Kevin said.

Anya had failed to notice that Loke was standing behind Kevin. She had not seen him since he had escaped from the Japanese. She clasped his hand and shook it with vigor. "It's so good to see you ... all of you. I can't thank you enough for finding me."

Mac felt a tug on his leg. He patted the boy on the head. "How in the hell did you and Jacob get together."

"That was a miracle," Anya said. "Wasn't it Jacob?"

Jacob tilted his head up and gave her a toothy grin.

"How did you manage to escape the Nips?" Kevin said.

"Their ruthlessness got them killed. You remember the village massacre?"

Kevin nodded.

"A slip of a village boy tracked them and took his revenge."

Mac scanned the area. "What is this place?"

"I call it Shangri-La," Anya said.

"What?"

"You know. Like the movie *Lost Horizon* where survivors discover a lost city in the Himalayas. Anyway ... you must be hungry. I'm suddenly starving."

THAT EVENING THE FIVE OF THEM CROWDED around a table barely able to accommodate three. Jacob sat on Mac's lap. Even though he had put Jacob down several times, Mac finally gave in. Anya had prepared rice and fish congee.

Mac stirred his food and looked up at Anya. "I'm sorry I got you into this mess."

Anya swallowed a bite of her meal. "How so?"

"I suggested they send you."

She shrugged. "I wasn't happy with the assignment, but I don't blame you. It was supposed to be a simple transfer."

"Still," Mac mumbled.

"How did you ever find me?"

"Kevin tried to get the local army involved, but they said they didn't have the manpower or some lame excuse so he and Loke decided to find you. They heard I was due to arrive in a few days and waited—three is better than two. Colonel Colson gave us all the supplies we needed. I think he felt bad leaving you without any protection when they dropped you off at the rendezvous. With the onslaught the Nips left in their wake, it was easy to follow their trail. We ran into a kid who said he had guided a woman and kids to this village."

"That was Bo, the village boy I was telling you about," Anya said. "So, what's the plan?"

"We head to Kunming. It's about a week's trek back through the bush," Loke said

Anya grimaced at the thought of returning to the jungle. "Can't we get a helicopter in here?"

"A what?"

"Helicopter. They used one to transfer an injured man out a few weeks ago."

"I've never heard of such a thing," Mac said.

Anya remembered Colson telling her it was an experimental operation.

"We didn't run into any patrols on the way so it should be relatively smooth sailing."

Anya's focus turned to Jacob. He had attached himself to Mac. Mac would have to break it to Jacob that he would not be accompanying them. She was not looking forward to that scene.

MORNING CAME EARLY FOR ANYA. SHE HAD taken a lengthy bath knowing it would be several days before she would be able to bathe again. She put on the jungle khaki uniform and boots the men had brought her.

Anya heard Jacob sobbing in the other room. Mac assured him he would return to visit when the war was over and he had completed his mission. Anya hoped Mac was being honest and not building up the boy's trust only to crush it later.

Anya and Mac walked Jacob to his new family. His adopted parents greeted them. The girls were shy and hid behind their adoptive mother's skirt. Anya could not tell if they remembered Mac, and he was not making any moves to encourage them. Jacob hugged Mac and then Anya one last time and took the hand of his adoptive father. Anya bit her lip to hold back her tears.

Anya had packed food and supplies and toted the weapons she had taken from the dead soldiers. Although she believed Mac when he said they had not run into the enemy, she was not taking any chances.

I will die before being taken prisoner again.

The village had turned out in force. Their smiles and waves did not fool Anya. She knew their joy was in seeing them leave.

Anya stopped to say goodbye to the old man. "I can't begin to thank you for all that you have done for me and the children."

The old man bowed. "If nothing else, humanity

must survive." He placed a piece of yellow jade in her hand. "This will protect you from harm."

"One day I will return. That's a promise." She placed the jade in her jacket pocket. Before Anya took her final step and disappeared into the jungle, she turned to face the village. A heaviness gripped her legs as though weights tied them down.

There is a sense of serenity in this little village that I've felt nowhere else. Even though it will be hard to give it up, I must return to my world, to find Joe, and retrieve my ring, but one day I will return.

"Are you all right?" Kevin said. He stretched his arm to her farthest shoulder, reminiscent of an embrace.

"I wanted to take one last look."

Mac strolled over. "Is there a problem?"

Anya sensed an irritation in his tone. "No, I'm ready." She turned and walked along the narrow path and once again entered the forest.

TWENTY-NINE

LOKE LED THE WAY FOLLOWED BY ANYA AND Kevin. Mac brought up the rear. The sun was high in the sky, but the usual sweltering heat had subsided. Anya's thoughts rolled back in time. *How long have I been in China? A month? Two? I've lost track. Seems like a lifetime.*

Loke raised his arm. Everyone halted and stood in silence. Anya's pulse raced at the sound of rustling in the brush. *That's all we need, a J-patrol.* She slowly removed the rifle from her shoulder and readied her weapon.

A dark blur bolted across their path.

Everyone flinched.

"Relax, it's a buck," Loke said.

Anya released a held breath. She heard the men behind her do the same.

"That'll get your adrenaline pumpin'," Kevin said.

"After all we've been through, I'm not sure I have much to spare," Anya said.

THE SHADOWS OF DUSK HAD DESCENDED AND they agreed to hole up until dawn. Anya stretched out on her blanket roll and listened to the whoop of monkeys, the grunt of boars, and the buzz of ever-present mosquitoes. She prayed the campfire would keep tigers away.

The glow from the fire allowed Anya to see Kevin's face. "Kevin," Anya lifted herself onto her elbows and winked, "you never did finish telling me about how you and Mac use to hang out at bars and try to pick up women."

"Oh—yeah. The ladies loved Mac."

Mac sighed. "Aren't you two tired?"

Anya fell back and giggled. Kevin's laugh reverberated.

Mac turned his back to the two clowns.

CLOUD COVER HAD ROLLED IN DURING THE night. The sweet pungent aroma of imminent rain filled the air and with it, humidity.

"Best get a move on before the rains come," Loke said. "If it's a drencher we'll need to seek shelter."

The stillness struck Anya. "It seems the animals sense it too."

They had not gone more than a few kilometers when the clouds let loose. The droplets were the size of pebbles. Rain bounced off their heads and backs with a force that felt like rocks.

"Hug a tree," Mac yelled. "Their branches will shield you."

Anya stood with her back against the widest tree and watched the water splat on the ground. She saw Kevin glance her way. She wondered if he too was recalling the time the Japanese forced them to stand out in the rain while they all took shelter. She had explained to PL that if they got sick, the soldiers would need to carry them. It was the last time they were forced to stand in the rain.

"I guess we won't need to worry about bathing for a while," Kevin said.

Anya twisted her hair to wring out the water. "I guess not."

As fast as the rain came, it quickly stopped, and they moved on. Anya lost her footing on the slick mud and fell on her bottom. "What was that you said about not needing a bath?"

Kevin was the first to help her up while Mac watched with a fixed eye. Kevin moved to help wipe off the mud.

Mac said. "I think she can manage on her own."

"Just trying to oblige, ol' man." Kevin winked.

They maneuvered their way along the path. It opened onto a rutted road. The three waited while Loke scouted ahead. Moments later, he motioned for them to advance.

"We can't use this road," Loke said. "It's laden with mines. I found one up ahead. We'll have to stay on the trail."

Anya had hoped the road was accessible. The tall brush scraped her hands and face, inviting insects to feast on her blood. They had not traveled far when Loke again raised his hand.

Not another deer, Anya thought. But this time she heard the familiar steps of soldiers. "It's J," she said.

"How do you know?" Loke said.

"I traveled with them long enough to recognize those short synchronized steps."

Time did not allow them to delve deep into the jungle before the enemy drew closer. They hit the ground, prostrated themselves, and lay in silence.

Anya thought her heart would explode from the pounding in her chest. Her left cheek rested on the still wet ground. She counted the legs of Japanese soldiers. Six pairs marched by. Suddenly one stopped. He turned their way and stared in Anya's direction. She tried to quell her trembling body for fear it might snap a twig under her. *Please.*

Please. Please. Don't anyone make a sound or do anything stupid. Their position and being out-manned made them vulnerable.

The soldier stepped off the path and headed her way. *What do I do?* Anya's mind reeled. She only had enough time to grab her rifle, sit up, and fire one shot. He was within steps but he stared ahead of her. *He doesn't see me. He's going to walk right on top of me.*

His foot was within a stride from her face. The whoop of a monkey echoed from behind. He stopped, pivoted, and returned to the path. He turned back toward her. A soldier came up from behind and nudged him to move on.

When their footsteps died out, Kevin jumped up. "I will never disrespect another monkey."

Loke turned to Anya "It was Mei."

"What do you mean?"

"Her spirit is with us, helping us." He walked into the brush to relieve himself.

Anya was hesitant to believe him, but in her heart, she ached for it to be true.

A voice boomed from the path. *"Ho-rudoappu"*

Anya raised her arms in surrender. She knew the Japanese word for hands up.

Anya glanced around. Mac and Kevin were on either side of her. *Where is Loke?*

THIRTY

Anya, Kevin, and Mac remained collected as the Japanese soldier marched forward with his steel bayonet poised to attack. Anya's eyes scanned the area in search of Loke. *We could use your stealthy guerrilla warfare right about now.*

She barely completed her thought when Loke darted out from behind a tree and lashed out at the enemy with a strike like a deadly adder. He wrapped one arm tight around the soldier's larynx lifting his chin upward. The other hand plunged a knife deep into the enemy's back. The soldier's knees buckled, and he crumpled to the ground. Mac and Kevin helped Loke throw the body into the heavy brush, but not before Mac confiscated the soldier's weapon. Anya and the three raced along the path. She hoped they would be safely away before the patrol discovered the body.

The quick pace began to wear on Anya. Her heart beat faster, her labored breath crackled, and her steps slowed. She felt she could not go on, but did not want to impede their progress. Yet, her body screamed, stop.

"I need to rest," Kevin said.

Anya noticed Kevin feigned short breaths. She was grateful to not have been the one to admit it.

"We can take a moment to rest, but we have to push on," Loke said. "There is a training camp a few hours ahead. They should be able to feed and put us for the night."

THE FEW HOURS LOKE PREDICTED TURNED INTO more than four as the pace had slowed to a measured walk. By the time they arrived at the camp, night had fallen. They entered to find that guards flanked them on all sides. Loke spoke one word, "*Pengyou*." The guards eased their weapons. One woke up the commander who recognized Loke and roused the cook to prepare a hot meal.

The moon was the only source of light aside from a single oil lantern. Anya managed to make out the silhouette of a few tents and a wooden structure. The food arrived, but the weight of the rice bowl was almost too much for Anya's arm to lift to her mouth. Her eyes were at half-mast as she chewed once before she swallowed. After the meal and without moving from her spot, Anya unrolled her bed and passed out.

THE MORNING SUNLIGHT DID NOT WAKE ANYA. It was the constant high-pitched clicks of something being struck. She opened one eye, then the other, and raised herself upright. Several meters beyond were a dozen or more children dressed in black tunics and pants. They were paired up, using long sticks to strike one another in combat practice. *They can't be much older than Jacob.*

"Morning." Kevin knelt and handed her a small bowl filled with hot tea.

Anya breathed in the flowery jasmine spice and took a sip. "Where are we?"

"Some type of training camp—for kids."

"Do you remember the Little Resisters that helped rescue you?"

He nodded.

"A camp like this is probably where they got their training."

Beyond the practice site stood a tall wooden structure. Several children climbed atop the apparatus while others swung from one bar to the next, reminiscent of monkeys in the trees.

"You must be Anya," a voice boomed overhead.

Anya covered her eyes and looked up to see a short, stocky man with a jet-black ponytail. Next to him were Mac and Loke. She stood, careful not to spill her tea. "Yes."

"Welcome. I'm the commander of this unit."

"You ready these boys and girls for battle?"

"It may seem immoral to you, but to win this war, we must recruit everyone willing to defend our country. We rely heavily on children as combatants, scouts, porters, spies, and informants. Most are trained to avoid contact with the enemy, but if the situation arises, they must know how to defend themselves to survive."

"I'm not judging what you do here, just trying to understand."

"Because they are small, they are more mobile. They become our eyes and ears in the bush. We Chinese live by the rule, if you only know yourself but not your opponent, you may win or lose. If you know neither yourself nor your enemy, you will always endanger yourself."

"I see you teach them self-defense," Mac said. "What else?"

"Some learn to fire at a target then quickly move to avoid counter-battery fire. You'd be surprised how many shoot better than most men."

"Some women too." Mac looked over at Anya who smiled.

"We use guerrilla warfare tactics," the commander said. "When the enemy camps, we harass. When the enemy tires, we attack. When the enemy retreats, we pursue."

Loke piped up. "Can you spare a meal before we are on our way?"

"I'll walk you over to the food station."

Some of the children followed closely, touching Mac's and Kevin's bare arms. They pulled away from the children.

The commander shooed them off. "They've never seen a white person. They want to see if you feel the same, especially white men with hairy arms. You see, we have beautifully smooth skin." He laughed.

They arrived at the food station where the cook dished up rice and water spinach.

"Do you know if any of our troops are around the area?" Loke said to the commander.

"About a week ago there was a unit over the mountains, a day's march northwest, but they may be fighting an enemy patrol who was also seen in the area."

"Aren't you worried about being captured?" Anya said.

"We have lookouts throughout the area. They knew you were coming hours before you arrived." He smiled. "If we need to, we simply pick up our sticks and move on. Everything else can be rebuilt."

A boy came up to the commander and whispered in his ear. The commander turned to Loke. "He wants to scout for you."

Loke turned to the group. "What do you think?"

"No way." Mac recoiled. "I don't want to be responsible."

"Mac," Anya said, "these children have survived for years in this manner. I think we should take all the help we can get."

"It's true," Kevin said. "They helped save my life."

"I think it's a bad idea but if you all agree, who am I?"

Anya spoke to the boy in Chinese "What is your name?"

"Hao Yong"

"Everyone, this is Hao."

The group picked up their gear. Hao led the way with a fierce determination on his face. They headed toward the mountains.

THIRTY-ONE

The dense, suffocating undergrowth of the jungle required Loke to machete their way through, aided by Anya's compass. The oxygen hung heavy, moist, and still. A sudden odor of rotting fruit hit Anya's nose. Her muscles tightened from the all too familiar smell. As they pressed on, the sharp stench grew stronger. Bile rose from her gut and she swallowed hard. She tried to mask the odor by shielding her nose with her jacket sleeve.

A small clearing exposed the remains of a battle, a graveyard of the unburied. Uniformed corpses from both sides strewn in heaps among the waves of green grass and weeds—many still gripped their weapons. The squawk from birds echoed as they tried to protect their claim of exposed soft flesh.

"We should check if any are alive," Anya said.

"There won't be," Loke said. "The wounded don't last long in this environment."

"We must be close to the Chinese Army," Mac said.

"Yeah," Kevin said. "And the enemy too."

Loke spoke to Hao, who then ran off. "I've asked him to scout ahead. Let's move on."

They hadn't walked more than an hour when Loke stopped and peer down the trail.

"What is it?" Anya said.

Loke placed his finger to his lips.

An odd chirp came from beyond the limits of their sight. Loke smiled and returned with a tweet of his own. "It's okay. It's friendly."

A Little Resisters, not Hao, came running toward them. Breathless, he spoke to Loke, who patted the boy on the shoulder and nodded. "He's been dispatched to tell us that the enemy, a dozen or more, are headed our way."

"It's probably from the unit whose soldier we killed," Mac said.

Kevin said with a quiver in his voice, "If I weren't so tired I'd say let's stand and fight, but we need to get out the hell out of here."

"Let's keep moving," Loke said. "Everybody be vigilant. The enemy may be in front of us as well."

They reached a stream where Hao sat on a

rock waiting. Hao saw the other LR and his face lit up. The two boys hugged as though they had not seen each other in years. Loke crouched next to Hao to talk. Anya, Kevin, and Mac each claimed a rock and rested.

Loke turned to the group. "Hao says he spotted a Japs camp about an hour directly ahead."

"Can we divert?" Mac said.

"We'll have to but that makes the trek much longer and more treacherous. Some of these mountains are rock-faced."

"We don't have the equipment to climb sheer cliffs," Mac said.

"There are manmade ledges, but it doesn't lessen the danger," Loke said.

"Maybe we should send the boys back," Anya said.

"Yes," Loke said. "There isn't much more they can do for us after we leave the bush."

Relief filled Anya at leaving the jungle behind, but a perilous mountain hike did not seem like a fair exchange.

Anya spied on the boys as Loke talked to them. She saw their bottom lips stick out from disappointment. Anya almost burst into laughter as Hao argued to remain. She almost wanted to give in to his demand but knew it was best he return.

Anya bent her head back so far it touched her back. "We have to climb up and over that?"

"It's that or be shot," Mac said.

Kevin said, "Being shot or bouncing from rock to rock as your body careens down the mountain face. Not sure what's worse."

They formed their usual lineup, Loke, Anya, and Kevin followed by Mac. The first several hours the terrain remained relatively easy. The wind picked up as they reached the timberline and the trail narrowed to the width of a single step. The loose, wet gravel felt like walking on ice.

"Is there anything at the top?" Anya said before she took a sip of water.

"Centuries ago," Loke said, "the local tribes believed an underworld god lived on the mountain. It became a place of pilgrimage. It was also an important place for immortality seekers as many herbal medicines and powerful drugs are reputed to be found there."

The pebbled trail ended. In its place, a suspended rope bridged two crags. Midway across, vertigo overcame Anya. Her moist palms gripped the sides of the rope to steady herself. "Everyone stop. I'm getting dizzy." The swaying motion on the bridge halted. "Loke, go ahead and cross. Kevin, please remain here until I get across."

"I know what you mean. I was starting to get

a bit queasy myself," Kevin said.

Anya gingerly crept across one step at a time to the other side. She wiped the hair from her face. "Sorry, I don't know what happened."

"I do," Mac said. "Remember the ship crossing when we first arrived? You spent most of the trip in your cabin."

"Oh, yeah. I forgot about that."

The higher they climbed, the more demanding each step became and their breathing labored. Anya felt confident about her climbing abilities until she saw the trail width decrease to half the size. An iron-linked chain had been hammered into the rock. It stretched several meters across. She clutched the chain for support and looked to the heavens. *Any slipup and I'm a goner.* She reached the end and turned to see Kevin's body slammed up against the rock face. His white knuckles gripped the chain as he inched his way forward.

"Keep steady ol' man," Mac said. "Take your time. You'll get through it."

Almost to the end, Kevin lost his footing. He clung to the chain as his legs dangled off the edge. Anya felt her face flush and extremities tingle as if she were going to faint.

"I've got you," Mac said. "Try to pull your legs up."

"My hands are slipping," Kevin cried out.

Loke stretched around Anya and went back to help Mac. Loke grabbed Kevin's upper arm and together he and Mac hoisted Kevin up so he could get the toe of his boots back on the narrow ledge.

Anya let out a sigh of relief when everyone was safely back on the wider ledge.

"I think my life passed before me," Kevin said with a nervous snicker.

"The good news is that we are almost to the top," Loke said. "The cliffs are only on this side, so the worst should be over."

"Hallelujah," Anya mumbled.

They reached the summit and Anya took a moment to scan across the vista. "It's like being on the roof of the world." A thin layer of mist hovered above the forest. Overhead, wispy strands of cirrus clouds swirled in the sky.

"We need to find a place to shelter for the night," Loke said.

Mac rushed toward them. "I can see their camps."

"Whose?" Loke said.

"The Chinese and the enemies. "From up here, you can see both positions. They are maybe 50 miles apart. We need to warn the Chinese."

"It will have to wait until morning," Loke said. "We need to rest." Loke found a pile of boulders that had formed a cave-like structure.

Exhausted, Anya collapsed next to Kevin. "Back there—I didn't realize that you were afraid of heights.

"It's an old bugaboo I can't seem to shake."

"But you pilot a plane."

"I feel safe and secure in a cockpit." He shrugged. "I know. I don't understand it myself."

"It seems you do much better in the air than on the ground," Anya said.

Loke turned to Anya and Kevin. "Has anyone seen Mac?"

Anya's jaw dropped. She remembered the time Mac had slipped away and she had to go after him in Chungking. "I have an awful feeling he went ahead to warn the Chinese."

THIRTY-TWO

ANYA AND KEVIN HUDDLED NEAR THE CAMPFIRE as Loke stoked it. He shook his head. "That fool's on his own."

"Talking about me?" Mac approached the fire and rubbed his hands together near the flames.

Anya's eyes widened. "We thought you'd gone ahead to warn the Chinese army."

"What made you think that?"

"You've done it before."

Mac returned a cheeky smile.

"Where have you been?" Kevin said.

"Monitoring the enemy. It's amazing how widely campfire illuminates the dark sky. Their stationary lights suggest they aren't moving. They may not know how close they are to each other."

"Or," Loke said, "biding their time for a surprise attack."

Mac scratched his stubbly chin. "Possibly."

"We'll reach the Chinese camp tomorrow," Loke said. "Until then, let's get some sleep."

THE NEXT MORNING ANYA WOKE TO A tangerine sunrise the width of the horizon. A crisp chill was a welcome antidote to musty humidity. Anya finished the last of her wild herbal tea and emptied the sediment on the ground. She slung one rifle over her shoulder and kept the other in her hands in anticipation of an enemy encounter.

The trek downhill was a gradual switchback. Mac kept his eye on the enemy camp until it disappeared from view. Soaring birds of prey and rabbits replaced parrots and monkeys. The air held the scent of pine, which reminded Anya of her childhood Christmases of roast goose, pierogi, and gingerbread cookies. Hunger poked her stomach.

It took hours to reach the basin and several more for them to cross a river and forge through a meadow. The sun had a few moments left before it melted into darkness as they reached the Chinese camp.

Two armed guards, guns drawn, stopped them at the outskirts of the camp. Loke approached the guards with his hands in the air. The others followed suit. Loke spoke to them in Mandarin.

Their eyes darted from him to the group and back to him. It seemed like hours to Anya before Loke turned to tell them the guards agreed to take them to the commander.

As they marched through the camp, soldiers in soiled faded khaki uniforms put aside what they were doing and watched them parade past. Anya heard their whispers. One questioned who they were, another guffawed and said lost tourists, a third said spies. She was glad Mac did not understand what they were saying, or he might have had a nasty retort to the spy reference. By the time they reached the commander's tent, they had amassed a troop of soldiers in tow.

The commander, a short barrel-chested man with pronounced cheekbones and a wide mouth strutted out to meet them. His chest was laden with a dozen ribbons and medals. Anya thought his large head looked out of proportion to his body. His focus darted past Kevin and Mac and stopped at Anya. He raised an eyebrow and pressed his lips together.

Loke bowed to the officer.

The commander spoke to Loke. "Who are these people?"

"They are Americans who got separated from their group."

Mac interrupted. "Tell him about the enemy

not more than 30 miles away."

Loke turned to Mac and glared at him.

The commander replied in English. "We know their whereabouts. I am Commander Delin, and you are?" He extended his hand.

"Mac. Mac Benson." Mac did not want to identify himself as a military man.

"Why are you in this area?"

Loke butted in. "We are merchants who were ambushed and have had to travel several days out of our way to avoid running into the enemy."

Delin remained quiet. Anya watched his eyes. He was examining them with careful deliberation. "Where are you headed?"

"Kunming."

Delin's eyebrows furrowed then released. "Stillwell's troops? That is several days march north from here."

Loke nodded. "Our food is in short supply. We'd appreciate any supplies you can afford."

Commander Delin ordered a soldier to assist in getting what supplies they needed. "Please join me in my tent for dinner tonight."

Loke bowed. "Thank you. We would be honored."

Mac sidled up to Loke as they walked to get supplies. "What was that lie all about?"

Loke stopped to address the group. "Do not

offer more information than I have already given this man. Even though he is an ally, he is a former warlord and still holds on to the belief that when the war is over he will regain his territory. He has no regard for anyone or anything except power. It is said that he has the brains of a pig and the temperament of a tiger."

AT DINNER, COMMANDER DELIN INSISTED ANYA sit next to him. Delin sat at the head with Anya on one side and Loke on the other. Mac sat between Anya and Kevin. Seven soldiers filled in to complete the table seating. At one point, Delin put his hand on Anya's leg. A chill ran through her spine and her body stiffened. She felt the blood rush from her face and turned to Mac. He placed his left arm around her shoulder exposing his wedding ring. A scowl crossed Delin's face and he ignored her the rest of the evening.

The meal consisted of meat and rice. From the sweet earthy aroma, Anya assumed it was a wild boar. There was an abundance of wine and loud conversation, the latter indistinguishable. At a certain point when the noise level reached a crescendo intensity, Delin raised his arm and the tent fell silent. This ebb and flow of clatter continued throughout dinner.

"Tell me, Mr. Benson," Delin said while chewing his food, "what brings you to China?"

Mac glanced across the table at Loke who sat frozen, lips parted ready to take a bite.

"I'm an importer. I—that is we," he nodded toward Anya, "came to China to initiate a business venture of importing items to the U.S. Army."

Loke placed the food in his mouth and chewed.

"What type of items?"

"Anything needed."

"I could use such a supplier."

"I'm sorry, but I'm under an exclusive contract with the U.S. government."

"I see." Delin turned to Loke. "It would be best if you were to leave before sunup."

"That was our plan, but why?" Loke said.

"At first light, we plan to seek out the enemy camp Mr. Benson mentioned."

THIRTY-THREE

Anya woke up groggy minutes before the sun breached the horizon. Yesterday's long trek and a restless night had taken a toll on what energy remained. The men slurped hot beverages as she sat upright and readied herself for the day. Kevin handed her a tin cup. A bitter metallic aftertaste lingered as she sipped the hot tea.

Loke said, "We should get a move on."

Anya rose to her feet. Before she was erect, a high-pitched rush of air flew past her ear. She froze. Her eyes darted over to Mac. A second later, they heard loud screeching from what sounded like a herald of banshees as a mob of Japanese soldiers swarmed into camp. Shots ricocheted off trees. The impact of a shot spun a Chinese soldier off his feet. Return fire exploded from the allies. Chaos consumed the camp as some men charged the invaders while others scrambled for cover.

Anya and the men dashed for their weapons. Adrenaline surged through her veins as she grabbed two rifles. She took a position behind a tree—half for protection, half to stabilize her aim. She managed to stop two of the enemy before they gained any advantage. To her right, she spotted Kevin in hand-to-hand combat. The butt of an enemy rifle struck him and knocked him to the ground. The soldier made ready to impale Kevin with his bayonet. Anya fired a clean shot. The soldier collapsed on top of Kevin, who threw the body off. He sprang to his feet and gave her a quick thank you salute. Kevin darted for the trees when another shot rang out. His knees buckled and he fell forward, prostrate, to the ground. A sharp pain pulsated in Anya's stomach as if someone had slugged her. Unaware the fighting had ended and disregarding her safety, she ran to Kevin's side.

"Don't you die on me." She flipped him over and a whimper passed from his lips. She moved her hands over his body to find the wound. "Where is it? Where the hell is it?"

Kevin took her hand and placed it on his left side below his ribs. Her fingers felt the hole. She slid her hand to his back where the bullet had passed through. "You're lucky. It looks like it missed any vital organs."

"Yeah," he winced. "I feel really lucky."

Anya looked up to see Mac and Loke along with a Chinese soldier who carried a khaki satchel with a red cross on the front.

Anya said. "We need to get him to a safe place."

Mac placed his hand on Anya's shoulder. "The fighting is over. It was a small unit, probably the ones who've been trailing us."

The medic sprinkled gunpowder on the wound and ignited it with a match. It flamed up for a couple of seconds before he put it out with a damp cloth. Kevin screamed then passed out. He turned him over and applied the same procedure to the backside wound.

Loke turned to Anya. "He has cauterized the wound but says he shouldn't walk for a few days."

Kevin regained consciousness, his eyes half-opened. "Leave me. I'll slow you down."

"No," Anya snapped back.

"I thought you were in a hurry to get to Kunming," Mac said.

Anya bit her lip. "We can't leave him. He needs a hospital."

"What do you propose?"

"I don't know" She raked her fingers through her hair. "We can use a cot to carry him. It's only a few days and it's less mountainous."

"No, leave me."

"Shut up, Kevin," Anya said. "This discussion is not open to you."

Mac shrugged.

"If we take him, it will be all the sooner he sees a doctor," Loke said.

"Agreed," Anya said.

THE CHINESE HAD MOVED SOUTH TO ATTACK the Japanese camp by the time the four headed north. Mac and Loke carried Kevin on the cot. They took a well-worn path below a canopy of dense brush, which provided cover from enemy aircraft. The trek to Kunming would take longer than Anya imagined as the men needed to rest more often.

They stopped alongside a stream to fish for dinner and to rest that night. Anya noted that the men were unusually quiet. She was uncertain if it was due to fatigue, or if each one was thinking about how their worlds would differ when they arrived in Kunming. Anya thought about Joe. She had last seen him in Chungking as he headed south chasing Sun. She fell asleep thinking about how to locate Joe.

THE NEXT MORNING, ANYA FOUND HERSELF surrounded by eight sharp spears pointed at her head. The bare-chested men with tattoos, which looked like two rams heads stacked upside down on top of the other glared, at her.

One man grunted and prodded her with his spear. Anya looked around to see Mac and Loke standing, their weapons in the tribesmen's hands. Kevin remained laying on his cot. Defenseless and outmanned, they were forced to march in a single file ahead of the tribesmen. Mac and Loke carted Kevin.

The intensity of the sun's heat increased as the day wore on. Anya removed her jacket to gasps and whispers from behind. The man with the most prominent tattoo grabbed Anya's arm. She struggled to free herself but his grip was too tight. He lifted her short sleeve to expose the butterfly tattoo on her upper arm. He released her and spoke in a language she did not understand. Anya looked over at Loke.

"I don't know this dialect," Loke said. "I think he wants to know where you got that mark."

"Qui," Anya said.

The man smiled. He lifted his spear to the others who raised their arms in unison and cheered.

Loke shrugged. "They must be from an offshoot or cousins of the Qui tribe."

The leader ordered the return of their weapons and motioned for everyone to follow. Two tribesmen took over toting Kevin.

Mac sidled up to Anya. "A tattoo. You surprise me."

"I sometimes surprise myself."

They arrived at a spot scarcely large enough to be considered a village. Straw huts circled a communal fire pit in the center. A dozen women and children had gathered to survey the strangers. The leader clapped twice then spoke to the women who scurried off.

A man, who looked as old as Methuselah with a face as wrinkled as a dried grape, doddered over to Kevin. His face was painted chalky-white making his black eyes appear twice their normal size giving him the appearance of a hobgoblin.

"Lo—Lo—Loke." Kevin tried to crawl away.

"Relax," Loke said. "He's what you Americans call a medicine man."

The medicine man danced and chanted. He held a wooden goblet above his head as if asking the gods to bless it. He finished his dance and gave Kevin the goblet. He motioned for him to drink.

"Go ahead," Anya said. "It might make you feel better."

"Yeah, but it might kill me." Kevin smelled the concoction and wrinkled his nose. The medicine man tilted the cup toward Kevin's lips. Kevin took a gulp, held it in his mouth, and swallowed. Within minutes, he fell asleep.

THAT EVENING THE MEN AND ANYA SAT AROUND a blazing fire as the tribal women and children served them a platter of sour, spicy fish atop a bed of rice. Each person, in turn, pulled off a section with their fingers and scooped up a bit of rice with the fish. They passed the dish around the circle until every bite had been consumed.

The leader took a swig from a gourd then handed it to Anya. The clear liquid had the smell of sweet-rotting fruit. The harsh fumes told her it was some type of distilled alcohol. She took a sip and passed it. Instead of a stinging bite like vodka, a subtle warmth traveled across her chest.

Anya rubbed a smooth stone in her pocket. It had been given to her by the old man from the other village. It seemed right that she present it to these people as a thank you. She placed the yellow jade into the hands of the tribal leader. Tears filled his eyes. He bowed to thank her as tears rolled down his cheeks.

The gourd was handed around the circle, Loke started to sing. Anya giggled. Mac sat upright without expression and scanned the circle. Her laughter grew louder as she watched Mac's stoic observation of the merriment. *I think the OSS has sucked all the fun out of him.*

THE NEXT MORNING EVERYONE WOKE THE WORSE for wear, except Kevin who stood and stretched. "What a glorious morning."

Anya and Loke moaned. Anya placed her arm over her eyes to block out the daylight. "I feel like someone used my head as a punching bag."

"I feel great," Kevin said. "That concoction they gave me was some kind of magic potion. You don't need to carry me. I feel good enough to walk."

Anya eyed Kevin hobble away. *Yeah, he can walk—like a toddler.* She glanced at Mac, who looked at her with that 'I told you so' expression. "What?"

Mac remained silent with a smirk slapped across his face.

Anya rose and staggered to a barrel of rainwater. She splashed the water on her face and over her head. The coolness helped to reduce the ache and clear her mind's fog.

Loke and Mac approached Anya. "What should we do about Kevin?" Loke said. "He refuses to be carried. Says he can walk."

"I guess we let him walk," she said.

"He'll slow us up," Mac said.

"We can't tie him down," she said.

Kevin approached the group. "You talkin' about me?"

"Are you sure you can keep up?" Anya said.

"Fit as a fiddle."

"Okay, gimp," Mac said. "Let's pack up and head for Kunming."

THIRTY-FOUR

The murmur of a nearby stream played like musical notes. Anya closed her eyes as the familiar three-four beat of a waltz swirled in her thoughts. She envisioned herself wearing an elegant white chiffon formal with her parents by her side. Young officers eyed her as she —A loud pop brought her back to reality.

Incandescent sparks exploded upward as Kevin sat cross-legged and poked with a stick at a burning campfire log. Curls of gray smoke danced toward the night sky. "Tomorrow I'll be on my way back to the States." He sighed. "After all of this—what we've been through—bullets whizzing overhead, being captured, in peril every minute of the day, what's it going to be like, immersed in a completely different reality?"

"You sound disheartened," Anya said.

"Somewhat." He interlaced his fingers, placed them behind his head, leaned back, and gazed into the distance. "I'm anxious to see friends and family but—I don't know—I'm reluctant."

"In what way?"

"The Navy hammered me like a copper kettle and forged a man." He paused. "I don't want to fall back into my old habits. The playboy drunk of Manhattan."

"We all have something in the past that caused shame. But if we face that demon head on, it makes us stronger, so when it rears its ugly head we can conquer it."

"You think?"

"I know my past no longer defines me. And these last few weeks makes me believe it doesn't define you either."

"Maybe I was supposed to die in that plane crash or as a prisoner. Maybe I shouldn't have lived." He paused "I can't see myself living a day in, day out lifestyle."

"You surely won't be home for more than a month before you're reassigned. You'll be seated in a cockpit dropping bombs in no time."

"Yeah, but what do I do for that month?" Kevin looked at Mac who lay motionless with his eyes fixed on the starlit sky.

Anya noted that Mac had refused to sit around

the fire and join in the conversation. *Maybe he's thinking about his wife and daughter.*

Loke returned to camp with a rabbit draped over his shoulder. Anya cringed as he disemboweled it. First, he removed the front legs and head, then sliced a hunting knife along the ribcage and pulled out the guts.

Anya resumed her focus on Kevin. A sudden snap caused her to jump. Her muscles tightened as she became aware of her surroundings. *Will I ever be able to simply relax?*

She glanced around to Loke. He cracked the backbone of the rabbit. She turned away. "Maybe while you're home you can find a nice girl."

"I thought I found one." He waggled his eyebrows.

Mac cleared his throat.

Anya knew his ahem was sarcasm and ignored it. "You're too old for me, Kevin." She chuckled.

"When I get home, I'm going straight to a little neighborhood restaurant that serves the best Osso Bucco in New York. I took Mac there once. Do you remember, Mac?"

"Yeah," Mac grunted.

Kevin leaned in and muttered, "What's wrong with him?"

Anya shrugged.

"What do you miss, Anya?"

"I miss Russia, my parents, and a good shot of vodka."

"Do you long to return home?"

"Home. Where is home? Everyone I knew is dead." She stared at the red flames.

"You know something funny?" Kevin scratched his head.

"What?"

"I use to smoke two packs a day. I haven't had a cigarette since my plane crashed. Um … I guess that means I've quit. Mother will be pleased."

Kevin continued, "Where are you bound for?"

Anya rubbed her knees with hands as leathery as an elephant's hide. "I'm off to find an old friend here in China."

Mac exhaled a groan.

"Be nice, Mac." Anya turned to Kevin. "He can't quite bring himself to forgive a certain party."

"What's so special about this friend?" Kevin said. "Should I be jealous?"

Anya rolled her eyes. "It's not so much him as what he might have for me."

"What do you mean?"

"A ring—a very special ring. Someone stole—in a way—stole it, and my friend is helping me get it back."

"What's so special about it?"

"The center stone, a red diamond, is cut in a

unique square shape surrounded by blue and white diamonds. It was a gift from my parents for my sixteenth birthday. It's all I have left of them and who I am. I want it back."

"What happened to your parents?"

Anya's gut twisted. "They were murdered—by the man who possesses my ring."

"Murdered? What happens once you find him?"

"I don't know." She twisted her ring finger. "I haven't thought that far in advance. But I know one thing. I will get my ring."

Loke had set up a makeshift rotisserie with v-shaped sticks on opposite ends outside the fire. He had skewered the meat with a stick and was roasting it. Juices sizzled as they hit the hot embers.

"Where will you go, Loke?" Kevin said.

"This is my country. I'll hook up with another guerilla group and continue to fight. This war has been going on for ages."

"What do you mean?" Kevin said. "We've only been fighting for a few years."

"For you, but for us, it began with the bombing in '37. Dismembered bodies littered across the landscape. Mountainous piles of gray rubble lay where buildings once stood. Those who survived faced starvation. I was lucky. I escaped to the countryside." Loke rotated the meat. "Our countries have a long history of conflict. I'm not sure we will ever see peace. But I do know one thing. Wars are won one bullet at a time."

Anya stoked the fire. "We are indebted to you for our lives."

"You owe me nothing. The fact that there is one less Jap patrol out there is payment enough."

Anya peered at Mac who remained focused on the sky. "Mac, is something wrong? You're so quiet. Not your usual blustery self."

"Just tired."

Anya didn't believe him but thought it best to not poke a bear. She caught the reflective glint of an eye in the brush. Kevin sat up. Above a couple of monkeys jumped between tree branches.

"They're curious," Loke said. "They won't come near for fear of the fire." He continued to rotate the meat.

The smells of skunky-gamey rabbit and musty smoke flooded the air. Even though the sight of its dismemberment was repugnant to Anya, her stomach grumbled and her mouth salivated. Their bellies would be full when they walked into the city the next day. Anya sensed their lives would change in ways she could not envision.

THIRTY-FIVE

KEVIN INSISTED HE COULD WALK AND REFUSED the stretcher. He limped up the hill assisted by Mac and Loke. Anya led with jumbled thoughts that crisscrossed as to how she would find Joe and her ring. The four stopped at the summit of a high ridge. The sun shone directly above. Below lay Kunming. Lush green mountains surrounded three sides of the low-lying basin. South of the urban city, a cerulean lake extended for miles.

Loke pointed toward the south end of town where an airstrip had been carved out of reddened earth. Several wooden buildings stood nearby. "That's the American army base. We should be there within the hour."

"Kevin, how are you holding up?" Mac said.

"My wound is oozing a bit, but I'll make it."

Anya noticed a pale red stain on his shirt. "Our

first stop will be a hospital."

They snaked down the dirt trail until they reached a paved road. Several jeeps and trucks loaded with American and Chinese soldiers whizzed past. Their dust caused the four to cover their noses and mouths. They passed the Stars and Stripes that hung outside Army headquarters. Farther down the road were the living quarters. They marched straight inside the building with a flag that displayed the Red Cross insignia. Inside the hospital, an orderly sat behind a small desk.

Kevin placed his hand over his wound and hobbled over to the seated corporal.

"May I help you?" the corporal said.

"My name is Lieutenant Kevin Jones. I've been a prisoner, escaped, and I require medical attention." Kevin removed his hand to bare his wet red-stained shirt and hand.

The corporal sprang from his chair knocking it to the floor. "Yes, Sir," he said with a salute. "I'll get a doctor right away." His hand shook as he picked up the phone and dialed. "I have a naval officer in need of immediate medical attention. Yes—Yes, ma'am." The corporal replaced the receiver in its cradle. "A nurse will be out to admit you."

"Thank you, Corporal." Kevin turned to the others. "I guess this is the end of our journey. I wish you the best in your quest. Thank you all for what you've done. Mother will be grateful."

Anya teared up and gave him a long hug. "Best of luck, Lieutenant. Don't forget your promise to yourself."

Kevin slapped a long kiss on her lips, which caused Anya to blush. "Take care of the ol' man." He tilted his head toward Mac.

Mac shook his head then Kevin's hand. "I'll see you back in the States."

Loke wished Kevin a safe return home.

A young buxom blonde dressed in white with a black stripe on her white cap pushed a squeaky wheelchair. "Lieutenant Jones?"

Kevin turned to Mac and gave him an exaggerated wink. "Right here, ma'am."

The three stood and watched as she wheeled Kevin down the hall. He raised his hand without turning and waved goodbye. The trio ventured outside.

Loke faced Anya and Mac. "I must also leave."

"Where to?" Anya said

"Back to the bush, to connect with the guerillas."

"I almost wish I were going with you."

"We could use you."

"Good hunting, ol' man." Mac vigorously shook his hand.

They watched Loke walk away.

"Last night around the campfire, you were unusually quiet. Was something wrong?"

"Kevin." Mac took a deep breath. "Don't get me wrong. The guy's like a brother, but he's a bit of a lounge lizard."

Anya smiled. "You were concerned about my honor?"

No response.

"I think that was more for your amusement than mine. I think Kevin Jones will be just fine. By the way, why did you come back to China?"

"Atwater told me you were missing. You're my partner and you leave no man er, woman, behind."

"Thank you. I know to leave your family must not have been easy."

Anya waited for a response. None was forthcoming.

Once Loke was out of sight, a sinking feeling of abandonment overcame Anya. She, Kevin, and Loke had been through so much together and now they were all taking different paths. *This must be how a mother feels when her children leave home.* "I suppose you'll be leaving now?"

"Not yet," Mac smiled. "First we need to get back your ring."

THIRTY-SIX

A BOOMING NOISE THUNDERED OVERHEAD. ANYA shielded her eyes and looked up. Several gray twin-engine planes flew south.

"B-25 bombers," Mac said.

"What?"

"It's the type Kevin went down in."

Anya cupped her ears as the aircraft passed. "I wonder what happened to his crew."

Mac waited for the noise to abate. "I don't think Kevin knows. It haunts him."

A shiver traveled through Anya. "I need to contact Atwater and let him know I'm alive."

A parade of uniformed men strolled by and gave them the once over. Anya overheard one of the men comment, "Looks like they've gone native."

"We must look a fright," Anya said.

"Probably smell, too," Mac said. "Let's get cleaned up before we meet with anyone."

Anya was permitted to use the nurses' quarters to wash. She borrowed a pair of khaki slacks and a white blouse from a nurse. She saw Mac outside in Navy summer whites sporting a pair of aviator sunglasses. *I have to admit he is extremely striking in that uniform.*

"What are you grinning at?" Mac said.

"Nice glasses." She giggled then composed herself. "Where can I contact Atwater?"

He handed her a gold-colored badge. "Put this on." Imprinted on the badge were the words, War Department Military Security.

"What's it for?"

"It will get us into a place where you can contact Atwater."

Mac led her to Army headquarters where they made their way to the basement. A burly marine sergeant with a rifle blocked the hallway. He looked them both over, stared at their badges, saluted Mac, and stepped aside.

They entered a colorless cinderblock room. Chinese, Indian, and French Indochina maps hung on every wall. Every available table held a typewriter. Electric wires connected to phones and teleprinters crisscrossed the ceiling. Several men with headsets sat hunched over taking down notes.

"Miss Pavlovitch," a voice bellowed.

Anya turned to her right. "Colonel Colson."

"I wasn't sure we'd ever see you again, Miss."

Anya smiled and looked at Mac. "The Colonel gave me a lift to the jungle."

"Good to see you again Commander." Mac took Colson's hand.

"What can we do for you?" Colson said.

"I need to contact Edmund Atwater," Anya said.

"Your boss, as I recall."

She nodded.

"Corporal, contact Atwater at Honolulu headquarters for Miss Pavlovitch."

The corporal staggered over to the phone.

"Is he all right?" Anya said.

"He's new to Kunming and has a touch of altitude sickness. It's over 6,000 feet here."

"We've been in the mountains for so long I guess we've acclimated."

"Miss Pavlovitch, I have Mr. Atwater for you." The corporal handed her the phone, covered his mouth, and rushed out of the room.

"Mr. Atwater, Anya Pavlovitch here." There was a long pause as she listened to her boss.

"Yes, sir—but—yes, sir—but—that may not be possible at the moment."

Another long pause.

"I will do my best, sir. Goodbye." Anya tightened her lips and addressed Mac. "It seems they have me scheduled on another assignment."

Mac's brow furrowed. "What do you mean another assignment?"

Anya rubbed the back of her neck. "He wasn't specific, just that I was to report to someone at Detachment 101 in a week."

Laughter came from across the room. "See this patch." Colonel Colson pointed to a badge in the shape of an arrow stitched on his left shoulder sleeve. The top had a sun on one side and a star on the other. Below were five red and white stripes. "Detachment 101 insignia. We'll have one sewn on a uniform for you."

"I appreciate that the War Department believes in my abilities, but I have business elsewhere, Sir."

"Miss Pavlovitch, I suggest you finish your business and report back here in a week. There's a war going on, you know."

"Yes, Sir." Anya's shoulders slumped. She shuffled out the door, up the basement stairs, and into daylight. "How am I suppose to find my ring in a week?" She clenched her hands into fists and ground her teeth.

"If we play our cards right the government can

help us," Mac said.

"How does playing cards help us?"

"It's a—never mind. These people monitor China like an elephant cow with her newborn. If Sun's around, we'll find him."

Anya snapped her fingers. "Let's go to the American consulate."

"Why?"

"You remember Joe worked at the Shanghai consulate."

"So?"

"He knows every attaché in China. If he has communicated with the consulate, they may know where to locate him. I know you have trust issues with Joe, but I hope you can put that aside."

"You've put a lot of faith in this kid. But at the first sign of trouble, he'll get my boot in his keister."

"It won't come to that."

"Okay. Let's get a vehicle and drive into town," Mac said.

"Sounds good. I've done a lifetime of walking."

MAC, BEING TALLER THAN THE AVERAGE soldier, scrunched into the driver's seat of the topless metal green jeep. His bent knees touched the steering wheel. Anya secured her hair in a bun before climbing in. She was happy that Mac was at the wheel. She would relax with her feet on the dash. However, the unforgiving suspension made her wish they had walked into town.

"Do you know where you're going?" Anya said.

"I got directions."

They approached the stone wall that surrounded Kunming. A towering gate stood at the entrance. The center tower had an extended red curved roof. Each corner turned upward reminiscent of a winged bird. Two narrower towers with similar winged roofs were positioned on either side. Several shops and eateries were pitched outside the wall. Mac had to drive at a sloth's pace to avoid hitting pedestrians.

A flower market with an array of brilliant colors lay on the other side of the gate. A densely populated core encompassed by industry and housing awaited them. The juxtaposition of tall, gray European style buildings alongside colorful multi-layered wood temples created a surreal scene. Unlike the other cities they had encountered, there were few scars of war. The crowded streets were paved with various sized stones. Car horns honked, jeeps blasted, and motor scooters beeped incessantly—all scurrying for positions on laneless roads.

Anya's palms grew hot. The hustle and bustle of the city caused her heart to race. She choked from the suffocating gas emissions. *I almost wish I were back in the jungle.*

"Are you all right?" Mac said.

"I've been away too long. I need to regain my city legs."

They crawled along streets that held a lingering aroma of cooked pork and vegetables. Unlike Shanghai and Chungking, only a few Chinese men wore European style suits. American and Chinese soldiers mingled with the locals. On one corner, a mass of children surrounded American soldiers who passed out gum and hard candies. They crossed over a bridge. Below were hundreds of sampans filled with various products from vegetables to firewood. They drove past a flagstone courtyard estate. Anya spotted an elaborately carved front door and a landscaped garden of magnolia trees and pink camellia blossoms. "Must be the Mayor's house." She laughed.

Mac rolled the jeep partially onto the sidewalk and pulled in front of a two-story building that looked to have stepped out of an old western movie. "This is the place."

THIRTY-SEVEN

ANYA AND MAC WALKED UP A FLIGHT OF STAIRS and entered the American consulate office. A young man with dark cropped hair sat behind a desk. "May I help you?" His slow manner and quiet voice gave the impression he was the studious type.

Mac said, "We'd like to speak to the Counsel General."

"Do you have an appointment?"

"No."

"What is the nature of your business?"

"We're looking for someone."

"Sir, we're not a missing persons bureau."

"Look you, little twerp. I don't have time for niceties. I want to speak to your boss."

The man's eyes widened, his chest expanded, and he huffed.

Anya stepped in front of Mac. "If you could

please summon your boss, it's urgent."

The young man dialed a number. "I have two people who wish to speak to the consul general." He cupped the receiver, whispered into it, and hung it up. "The consul is not here at the present but his assistant will see you. Please have a seat."

Moments later a tall man wearing a brown double-breasted suit entered the lobby. "Hello, I'm Charles Huntsman. How can I help you?"

"Anya Pavlovitch and this is Commander Benson. We are trying to find a person who may be in the area. He worked at the consulate in Shanghai. It's paramount that I reach him."

"Is that a Russian accent I detect?"

"I work for the U.S. War Department. Is there a problem?" Anya recalled the same encounter with her nationality at the consulate in Chungking.

"No." Huntsman eyed Mac in uniform. "Let's step into my office."

Huntsman sat behind an uncluttered desk while Anya and Mac took seats directly in front.

"Who?"

"His name is Joe ... You know ... I don't know his last name." She turned to Mac.

"Don't look at me."

"You're looking for someone and you only know his first name?"

Anya took a deep breath. "He's in his twenties,

about my height, slender, Chinese. He was Sheldon Beaumont's assistant in Shanghai."

"Shelley, poor soul. The rumor was someone murdered him."

"It was never proven," Anya said. "Do you remember Joe?"

"Yes, I do. In fact, he came to this very office not more than a week ago."

Anya's heart pounded. "He's here? She sat at the edge of her chair. "Do you know where he is?"

"I do."

Anya stood up. "Why was he here? What did he say? Can you take us to him?"

"Hold on." Huntsman raised his forearm. "Why are you searching for him?"

Anya sat back down. "He's helping me locate someone."

"Would that be a criminal by the name of Sun Temujin?"

Anya bounced to her feet again. "Is Sun here?"

He smiled. "I'll let Joe fill you in."

ANYA PILED INTO THE BACK OF THE JEEP WHILE Mac drove and Huntsman directed him. They zigzagged around the city making left and right turns until they came to a continuous group of row houses.

"This is it. Number ten," Huntsman said.

Anya climbed over Huntsman who was too slow for her in getting out. She was the first to reach the front door.

The door opened and there stood Joe, skinny as ever, but to Anya, he looked wonderful. Without a word, she embraced him. "I can't believe we found you. In Kunming of all places."

"How did you find me?"

"Huntsman helped us," Mac said.

Anya hunted around the room. "Where's the dog?"

"He deserted me for the love of a little boy."

"I'm sorry."

"I think he was tired of traveling and wanted to stay in one place."

Anya saw a bit of sadness in his eyes.

"Come in. I'll fix some tea," Joe said.

"Never mind tea." Anya sat on the lumpy sofa. Mac and Huntsman followed. "Tell me everything since we last spoke."

"Sun headed north as we thought then veered south for some reason." He shrugged. "I think he's heading for India. It's the logical next step from Kunming."

"I think we'd have a better chance of nabbing him here than in India," Mac said.

"Agreed," Anya said. "We need to find him

before he secures transportation."

"I don't think we have to worry about him leaving right away," Joe said.

"Why?"

"It seems Sun could not control his wicked ways or needed money fast. Anyway, he stole something from a ruthless gang here in Kunming."

"Do they have him?"

"The word on the street is that he's in hiding."

"Do you know what he stole?" Anya said.

"It must be of great value because no one is talking."

Anya turned to Huntsman who shrugged.

"Maybe Colson can help."

THIRTY-EIGHT

ANYA AND MAC RETURNED TO THE BASEMENT and found Colson on the phone. Anya paced, twisted her ring finger, and occasionally glanced at Colson. Mac studied the maps that hung on the wall. Colson barely placed the receiver in the cradle before Anya pounced.

"We need your help." Her voice zipped at breakneck speed.

"Back up and slow down," Colson said. "Take a deep breath and start again."

Anya embarked at a measured rate. "Sun's in hot water with a local gang and hiding. I need you to work your spy magic and locate him."

Mac rolled his eyes.

Colson laughed, "It's not magic. It's painstaking, nose to the ground intelligence."

Anya felt her face flush. "Can you find him?"

"To tell you the truth, I don't have the manpower to help." Colson held up his hands. "Hold on before you get crazed. Your best bet is for you to contact the gang. If Sun has something they want, then together you might be able to assist each other."

"My enemy's enemy is my friend," Mac said.

"Exactly." Colson leaned back in his chair.

"How am I supposed to know how or who they are?" Anya said.

"There's one main syndicate in Kunming. They deal in stolen property, mostly medical supplies, and sell it on the black market. We've tried to nab them but quite honestly, I have a higher priority."

"Burma?" Mac said. "We saw the planes heading south and by what I see on the map, it's quite an extensive campaign."

"Yes. It's vital we push the Nips back to the sea before they settle in southwest China and cross into India."

"Who buys black market drugs?" Anya said.

"Doctors, clinics, anyone who needs medicine."

"What about this gang? How do I contact them?"

"The leader goes by the name of Zhu. We don't have a detailed dossier on him, but we do know that he's missing his right hand. Apparently, he was caught with his hand in the proverbial cookie jar."

"Do you know where he hangs out?"

"If we knew that, don't you think we would have arrested him?"

Anya's face flushed. "Any suggestions about where to start?"

"He's a cautious fellow. He won't come out of hiding for Westerners." Colson looked at Mac. "Especially one in uniform."

"I'll find something more suitable," Mac said.

"We've got a man on the ground." Anya thought of Joe.

"You know where the Market is at the south gate?"

Anya nodded. She remembered the bright colored flowers when they first entered the city.

"Have your man pose as someone desperate to acquire medical supplies and see if you get a bite."

"Sounds plausible. Thanks," Anya said.

"Don't forget, you're due back here in a week."

Anya mumbled to herself as she and Mac walked out the door. They climbed into the jeep and headed back to Joe's place.

JOE HAD FIXED BLACK TEA FOR EVERYONE. A sweet floral fragrance lingered as they sat around the table and sipped their drinks. Except for Mac, who took a slug of hooch from a flask he had acquired back at base.

"Joe," Anya said. "I need to draw out the head of the gang that's probably after Sun. Do you think you can pose as someone in need of medical supplies?

Joe swallowed hard and stared at her.

"I know it's a bit risky, but we need your help if we're to find Sun."

"Okay. For you I will." Joe wrapped his arms around his stomach and lowered his head.

Anya patted Joe's shoulder. "You'll be all right."

Mac took another swing from the flask. "We'll be within sight of you in case anything goes wrong."

Joe exhaled, relaxed, and picked up his teacup. "What do you want me to do?" He took a sip.

Anya said, "We'll go to the flower market tomorrow. Apparently, smugglers traffic in the shadows there. You'll ask around for basic supplies like bandages, needles, and medicine for some orphan children who need medical attention."

"What children?" Joe said.

"There are no children. We're pretending."

"Oh."

"Can you do this for me?"

Joe nodded.

"Great. Let's all get some rest. Tomorrow is going to be a busy day." Joe was the only Chinese Anya could trust, but she was concerned if he could pull it off given his trepidations.

Anya and Mac lagged behind Joe as he entered the flower market. Anya purchased a bouquet of flowers and carried them around pretending to shop while keeping one eye on Joe. Mac had changed into brown slacks and a white shirt to blend into the crowd, but there was no easy way to conceal a six-foot-two Caucasian in China.

From Anya's vantage point, she watched Joe move from vendor to vendor asking his questions. "I wonder how he's coming off. Maybe we should have rehearsed."

"He's doing fine," Mac said. "Look to the left. There is a man in black smoking a cigarette. He's been watching Joe."

"Do you think that's one of them?"

"That would be my guess."

"Why do you think Sun is dealing in stolen medical supplies?" Anya said.

"Most likely, he needs some fast cash to bribe people when crossing the border."

"Do you think he's sold my ring?"

"No. He'll need it to reestablish himself."

Anya gripped Mac's forearm. "The man in black is moving toward Joe. What should we do?"

"We need to let it play out. If you rush over there you could scare him off or worse—get Joe killed."

Anya's heart pounded.

Joe stood frozen as a man in black approached. He inched his way closer. Anya's hands pressed together, crushing the flowers she carried.

"They're just talking. If he meant him harm, he'd be dead," Mac said.

Joe looked at Anya. She and Mac quickly turned their backs to hide their faces. Anya swiveled around to see the man walk away. She took a step forward, but Mac held her back

"Slow down, Sister."

The man turned and flagged Joe to follow him.

"Now what?" Anya said.

"We trail 'em."

The two followed, staying well behind. They entered a dark tunnel with a faint light at the other end. Anya heard the scratching of rat's claws as they sped past. She thought she heard a squeamish sound pass Mac's lips. The two stepped into the light to find themselves surrounded by three-story buildings and no trace of Joe or anyone else.

THIRTY-NINE

MAC PULLED A PISTOL FROM HIS ANKLE HOLSTER. He continued forward with his weapon scanning the alleyway. Anya crept behind, along a narrow jumble of ramshackle buildings. *Not sure what's more vulnerable, leading or following. A bullet can come from any direction in this maze.*

Making a hairpin turn, they encountered a dozen gang members dressed in black. The tallest of the men chewed on a stick of gum as if it was his only meal of the day. His face was as weathered and wrinkled as a sundried prune. He dragged Joe in front and pointed a pistol at his temple. Anya raised her arm as to surrender and spoke to him in Mandarin.

"We are here in peace. We've come to meet with your honorable leader, Zhu."

"Who is with you?" The man removed the gun from Joe's head and waved it at Mac.

"A friend." Anya leaned toward Mac and from the corner of her mouth said, "Holster your gun."

Mac put his gun away and raised his hands.

Prune's eyes narrowed. "He looks military."

"We're not here to arrest anyone. We're here to help you."

"What makes you think we need your help?"

"Sun Temujin?"

Prune stopped chewing his gum.

"Please take us to Zhu."

Everyone stood frozen momentarily, then Prune motioned for Anya and Mac to follow. Anya approached the group and headed straight for Joe.

"Are you all right?"

Shoulders slumped, head bowed, Joe nodded.

Anya, Mac, and Joe were sandwiched between Prune and the rest of the gang with no means of escape.

They entered a wooden building and walked up three flights of stairs. Prune signaled for them to stay. He removed his gum and stuck it on the outside wall then entered a room at the end of the hall.

Anya looked at Mac who had his arms tight across his chest. Joe chewed on a fingernail. "Well, this is what we're here for." She heard voices but was unable to make out what they were saying.

The door opened. Prune motioned for Anya. Mac and Joe stepped forward, but Prune held up one hand while he ushered Anya in with the other.

"I'll be all right, Mac."

Inside sat a sizeable man dressed in a dark blue western-style suit. He rested behind a massive black lacquered desk. Anya noticed that at the end of his right jacket sleeve he was missing a hand. Zhu gestured for her to sit with his left hand.

"Who are you?" Zhu said.

"I am in search of the person who insulted you."

"Insulted me?"

"He stole something from you."

"No one steals from Zhu."

"Let's say he took the liberty to borrow something and forgot to return it. How will it appear to others if that person is not punished?"

Zhu's penetrating dark cold eyes stared at her.

A nervous tingle ran through her. *Have I said too much?*

"How do you know we have not already recovered the item?" Zhu said.

"I don't believe you have. Furthermore, I don't think you even know what he looks like, but I do."

"Why do you want this man?"

"He borrowed something of mine."

Zhu sustained his unblinking stare.

"I believe we can help each other obtain what is rightfully ours." Anya knew the medical supplies were not legally his, but when dealing with the head of a ruthless gang she knew one should be diplomatic and not quibble about semantics.

Zhu addressed Prune, who stood behind her, in a dialect Anya did not understand.

"My man here will take you to a place where you and your friends can stay."

"Thank you, but we already have accommodations.

"I insist."

"Very well." Anya rose from her seat. "Thank you."

Anya rejoined Mac and Joe.

"What did he say?" Mac said.

"I believe we've been initiated as members of this gang."

Prune took Anya aside. "Zhu failed to tell you there is a rumor that someone amongst us may be helping this man you seek."

"Who?"

"Someone close to Zhu. However, an accusation without proof could mean death. But when he slips up, I will be there to catch him."

Anya, Mac, and Joe followed Prune to a three-story structure. Red apartment doors along the exterior corridor faced a common area. Laundry dangled over balconies and fluttered in the wind like flags.

"This place is tinder ready for a spark to ignite the whole ball of wax," Mac said.

Anya sighed, "Well, let's hope we're not in it when it goes up."

They entered a flat on the second floor. It was a cold, cheerless room. A musty odor like an old basement hit Anya as she entered. The interior held two dingy davenports and a long table marked with several white-ringed stains. To the left was a hot plate on a counter and farther down, an enclosed bathroom. Two adjacent paned windows overlooked the flower market.

"This is perfect." Anya pulled the yellow-stained curtain back. "We can watch Joe from here."

"Speaking of which," Joe said. "What's the plan?"

Anya said, "Since it's medical supplies that were stolen, we'll have you pose as a doctor who needs sulfa drugs and penicillin for a Chinese orphanage that you manage several miles away."

"What if he asks me a medical question?" Joe said.

"He won't. He's only interested in making a sale," Mac said.

"You'll ask around the market to see if anyone has medicine," Anya said. "If they point you to the gang, tell them that they don't have what you need and ask if they know of anyone else who can help." Anya patted Joe's shoulder. "We will be watching everything. Any trouble and we'll be there in a flash."

Joe nodded.

Anya empathized with Joe's anxiety but knew it was the only way to flush Sun out into the open.

"Let's all get some shuteye," Mac said. "We have a long hard day ahead of us tomorrow."

Anya tried to sleep but thoughts of seizing Sun and retrieving her ring danced in her head.

ANYA STOOD AT THE WINDOW OF THE APARTment and peered through binoculars targeted at the bustle of the morning market. "Mac, do you see Joe?"

"Yeah, look to the right. He's in front of the yellow flower stand, talking to a guy."

"Got him."

They watched Joe move from one vendor to the next. The vendors all shook their heads except for one, who pointed to a meat cart, but Joe shook his head.

"I don't think he's having any luck finding our man," Anya said.

"I've been watching someone in the shadows. He's stalking Joe."

"Is it Sun?"

"Too tall."

"I'll bet it's Zhu's traitor."

"I'm going to take a closer look." Mac set his binoculars down.

"I'm right behind you."

FORTY

MAC POSITIONED HIMSELF CLOSE TO THE shadowy figure but far enough away not to spook him. Anya pretended to admire colorful silk fabrics strewn across a table. She paralleled Mac and continued to shop. *I wish I could get within range to see what this guy looks like.*

A vendor with a bundle of white camellias in his hands approached Mac. The vendor shouted at him in an annoying, squeaky, high-pitched tone. The noise caused the suspect to turn. Mac made eye contact with him. He gave Mac a scornful glare and bolted. Mac pushed the vendor aside and chased after him. The vendor tried to stop Anya but she knocked him down and chased after Mac, leaving Joe behind.

The three raced down an alleyway. Anya reached the end. It opened up to a street jampacked with bicycles, rickshaws, motorbikes, and hordes of people. She lost sight of Mac for a moment then saw his head and shoulders towering above the crowd. *Thank God he's tall.* She pushed her way through the mass as though swimming through a riptide.

Out of breath, Anya caught up with Mac at a four-way intersection. "Where—where is he?"

"I lost him. Damn it." He stuffed his hands into his pockets and kicked the ground.

"Did you get a good look at him?"

"He's definitely Chinese."

"Not funny."

"He's about five-six, five-seven. I never got close enough to the wiry bastard to see anything more than his ears stuck out like an elephant's."

"Let's go find Joe. Maybe he has something for us," Anya said.

They turned a corner and halfway down the block, a man with large protruding ears faced them. His eyes widened.

"That's him," Mac shouted.

The suspicious character took off.

Anya followed in Mac's wake of fallen pedestrians and cyclists.

The assailant pushed a vendor's cart in Mac's path. He went down with a shoulder roll but managed to bounce up into a running sprint.

Doesn't that guy know you can't keep a good man down? The hairs at the back of Anya's neck were soaked from sweat and her legs were tiring. *I wish this guy would fall.*

The thought barely left her mind when the man tripped. Mac caught up with him, dove at the man, and grabbed both legs. The man wiggled one leg loose and kicked Mac in the face. Mac lost his grip. The man jumped up before Anya could catch up and took off again.

Anya saw blood seeping from Mac's nose. He wiped his nose on his sleeve and pursued. She wanted to shout for him to stop and forget it, but she knew her plea would be ignored. Her legs yielded to fatigue. She quit the chase and hailed a rickshaw to take her back to the market.

MAC'S BREATHING BECAME LABORED BUT HE refused to give in. He hoped the other guy would tire, but to no avail. *It's like he has an electric cattle prod up his butt.*

The suspect ran into a building with Mac in pursuit. Mac reached the roof but lost sight of him. *Where the hell is he?* He circled then spotted him on an adjacent building. The man stood bent over, inhaling and exhaling. Mac used the time to rest also as they kept a close eye on each other. Mac glimpsed a hint of a smile across the man's face. Mac's eyes narrowed and he made a dash and jumped onto the roof of the other building. The man was more than two flights of stairs ahead of him by the time Mac landed.

Damn, I know I'm going to lose him if I can't catch him before he exits the building. Mac skipped multiple stairs as he descended. He failed to see the body lying on the ground until he was on the last step. It was halfway out the main door. *Christ, did he have a heart attack?*

Prune peered from around the corner massaging his fist, chewing and snapping gum.

"Nice job, ol' man." Mac patted Prune on the shoulder.

Prune hailed a man in a horse-drawn cart and bartered with the owner. Mac was skeptical if it was money or a threat the man received. They picked up the limp body, and all three crammed into the cart.

ANYA AND JOE RETURNED TO THE APARTMENT and rested on the couch. They sipped cold drinks. A vase of jasmine she had purchased to mask the musty smell of the room sat on the coffee table.

"Did you find out anything?" Anya took a sip.

"Only that if they know anything, most are too

afraid to come forward."

She set her drink down. "Hopefully Mac caught the man who was watching you."

"What man?"

"Oh, you didn't see him? I don't think he would have harmed you. He was probably trying to find out who you were them report back to Sun."

"I guess we got their attention. What's next?"

"We try again. Maybe this time Sun will pop his ugly little head out."

"Then we'll chop it off." Joe laughed.

Anya chuckled. "Let's get my ring first."

Their laughter ceased when they heard heavy footsteps outside the door. Anya and Joe sat frozen. Anya whispered, "That doesn't sound like Mac." The doorknob squeaked as it turned. Anya covered her mouth. *I forgot to lock the door.*

FORTY-ONE

THE APARTMENT DOOR SQUEAKED OPEN. ANYA'S heart pounded. She sat on the edge of her seat. Creak—creak—creak. The door opened and there stood Zhu. The sleeve of his handless arm stuck in a coat pocket.

Anya exhaled. "You scared the liver and lights out of me."

"Me too." Joe's voice quavered.

Without a word of apology, Zhu swaggered into the room and sat. "Wanted to see how things were going."

Joe bounced up. "Can I get you hot tea or a cold beverage?"

"Tea."

"We managed to give someone a chase, but I'm afraid we lost him," Anya said.

"Really." He raised an eyebrow of skepticism.

"Do you know something I don't?"

Zhu returned a sly smiled.

Joe placed the tea in front of Zhu and sat next to Anya. Zhu picked up the tea and took a sip. He was about to speak when a clamor outside the door diverted their attention. The door crashed open. Mac stomped into the room followed by Prune carrying a body over his shoulder.

Anya jumped to her feet. "Is he dead?"

"No," Mac said. "Out cold."

Prune dropped the body on the floor in front of Zhu. "There's your protégé."

Zhu clenched his jaw. Redness washed across his face. "Get a chair and tie him to it. You," he pointed to Joe, "get some cold water."

Anya's stomach churned. She knew what these men were capable of and wanted to flee, but her legs failed to move. She collapsed onto the sofa.

Joe handed the water to Zhu. He flung it at the unconscious man. The man moaned and raised his head. His eyes barely open, he scanned the room. He focused on Zhu as he tried to wiggle free. The secured rope held him in place.

Bile rose in Anya's throat at the panicked expression on the man's face. Her fingers pulled at her trousers. She felt Joe nudge against her as if looking for protection.

The man spewed words of apology and

forgiveness with a promise to repent. Zhu stared down at him. "Oh, you'll repent. I have plans for you—you traitor." He swung hard and slapped the man's face with the palm of his hand. The man's cheek turned crimson and began to puff up.

"If we didn't need you ... I ... I'd gut you here and now."

The man whimpered. "Anything. Anything, my Lord."

"After the swelling dissipates, give him instructions and set him loose." Zhu stormed out the door, slamming it behind him.

Anya felt the entire room relax with Zhu out of the picture. Joe collapsed back in his seat.

"I could sure use a shot of vodka," Anya murmured.

Prune stood close to the man. His hands balled up into fists.

Mac touched Prune's shoulder. "Don't do it. We can't have him show up to Sun all bruised and battered."

"Anya," Mac said. "Tell him what I said."

She translated Mac's warning. Prune grunted and walked away.

"Now what?" Anya said.

"Now the fun begins," Mac said.

"Fun for whom?" Anya said.

Mac tilted his head. "Traitor, over here. We'll

use the same plan, only this time we don't need to search for Sun because the traitor will take us right to him."

"Can we at least untie him?"

Mac scoffed. "You really are naive. I don't care how much pleading he did in front of Zhu. The first chance he gets, he'll take off. He stays tied up."

"What makes you think he won't run off when we let him go?"

"Prune will be his guardian angel."

"Miss Anya." Joe twisted his hands. "Can you tell me again what I'm to say to Sun?"

"You are going to tell him you need medical supplies for an orphanage several miles away and you have money to pay. We will give you a pouch stuffed with paper to appear like a bag of cash."

"What if he wants to see the money?"

"It doesn't matter. By that time, we'll have already surrounded him. When you hear Mac's voice, drop to the ground to avoid gunfire."

Joe swallowed hard. "Gunfire?"

"Look, kid," Mac said. "You'll be fine. Sun's more of a knifeman than a gunman. Just stay away from his cane."

"I don't think that's very reassuring," Anya said.

"He'll be fine. Everyone gets a bit jumpy before a mission." Mac winked at Joe.

"I'll be okay," Joe said.

"I know you will." Anya knew her words felt hollow. She hoped the plan would go without a hitch, but she also knew the possibility of a mishap and that someone could die.

FORTY-TWO

THE NIGHT HAD GIVEN ANYA ZERO RELIEF. HER mind could not relax and deep sleep never transpired. Her stomach turned at the prospect of seeing Sun later that day. She took a sip of tea to help moisten the dryness in her mouth.

What will I do when I see him?

"It's time," Mac said. "Everyone knows their part—right? Joe, take this satchel. Remember, you are pretending to purchase medical supplies. Anya and I will back you up."

"What about this guy?" Joe pointed to Prune.

"He knows what to do."

Anya addressed the group. "The hope is not to kill but capture Sun."

Everyone nodded.

Anya saw the expression on the traitor's face

and believed he had acquiesced to his situation. Compelled to be a double agent meant he was the least likely to survive. *But I'm willing to sacrifice anyone or anything to get my ring back.*

The group made their way slowly down the stairs of the apartment to the street. An overcast morning sky seemed to befit the mood of someone on their way to the gallows.

Joe and Traitor walked ahead with Prune strategically behind to ensure the traitor's compliance. Anya and Mac meandered through the market pretending to shop. The fragrant smells of fresh-cut flowers sweetened the air as they snaked their way around the booths. Anya's focus was on Prune as they walked along a crowded, noisy street with sounds of bicycle bells and beeping horns. She knew that if they lost sight of Joe, Prune would not. Prune turned a corner and fell out of sight. She and Mac picked up their pace.

"I feel like I'm back in the jungle—marching," Anya said. "Where is he taking us?"

"You know Sun. He likes remote quiet places where he can top off people."

Anya recalled finding Mac strung up in an abandoned building in Shanghai. Sun had tortured him for days.

"This time he's the intended victim." A smile spread across Mac's face.

"I can hardly wait to see the astonishment in Sun's eyes when he sees us," Anya said.

"He may not be that surprised. People who live with their eyes in the back of their heads have an acute sense of being pursued. He's probably aware of our presence."

Anya's chest tightened as she twisted her ring finger.

"His capture won't be easy. He's a solitary animal who lives in the shadows. He is acutely aware of his surroundings and gets spooked at the drop of a pin."

"You make this plan sound improbable if not impossible."

"As long as you know your opponent, you can outmaneuver him. The spy game is like playing chess. We have our pawns in front, along with our knight, and closing in are the king and queen."

"I'm not crazy about Joe being used as a pawn."

"Not all pawns are taken when the game ends." Mac stopped. "What did I tell you."

Anya looked ahead to see that they had been led to an abandoned part of town. Several bombed-out buildings stretched the length of the street. On the other side flowed a muddy river. She watched as Prune swing around to the other side of the building.

"Are you ready?" Mac said.

"Ready, King," Anya removed the gun from the small of her back and tightened her hand around the grip.

"Let's go, Queen."

Indistinguishable sounds echoed as the two entered the building. Angry voices became clear as Anya moved in closer. Through a stack of wooden pallets, she recognized the familiar scar that stretched from the top of his hairline down his cheek. *At last, I have you in my sights Sun Temujin.*

"Jesus, he's a mess," Mac said. "The first time I met that guy, he was Mr. Dapper, impeccably dressed in a blue suit and sporting a tiepin and twirling his cane. Now, look at him—greasy hair, tattered clothes. He looks like he has aged ten years since we last saw him. I guess that's what happens when you're on the lam. It takes a toll on your body."

"Yeah, I know," Anya said. "Sun appears upset that the traitor has brought Joe. Joe is trying to explain that he has money to pay for the medicine. Sun is demanding to see the money but Joe wants to see the drugs first."

"Smart. He may make an agent yet," Mac said.

"Uh-oh."

"What?"

"Sun seems to recognize Joe and asked him if

he's from Shanghai."

Joe glanced over toward Anya and Mac. "Don't look over here you idiot," Mac mumbled. "Where's our knight?"

Anya scanned the area. "He's directly across from us in position."

Sun turned toward Anya and Mac's direction and took a step back. Before anyone could make a move on Sun, he bolted. Mac and Prune took off after him.

"Sorry Miss Anya, but I didn't know what to do when he confronted me."

"It's okay. We'll get him."

Out of the corner of her eye, Anya saw that the traitor had collapsed onto the ground wailing with his face in his hands. "Poor old sod. He has to face Zhu."

Anya searched the warehouse and found a crumpled blanket on a cot. Empty ration cans lay scattered about. "What a pig." Movement under the blanket caused her to lift the edge with two fingers. A black rat stuck its head out, hissed at her, and dashed off.

Anya jumped back with a yelp.

Joe came running over. "Are you all right?"

"Found a bedfellow."

She continued to rummage through Sun's things. She found a piece of paper with dates and times and stuck it in her pocket. She spotted a crate in a corner.

Mac and Prune had returned empty-handed. "Jesus, he's a slippery S.O.B.," Mac said. "A perfectly good plan shot to hell."

"Not all is lost." Anya lifted the lid of a crate. Inside were bottles, boxes, and bags of supplies marked, Property of U.S. Army.

Prune peered into the box with a smile

Anya barked at him and Prune's smile vanished.

"What did you say to him?" Mac said.

"That fine old American expression—finders keepers."

Mac laughed.

"Look what else I found." Anya handed Mac the slip of paper. "I can't figure it out."

"I know what it is."

"What?"

"Flight schedules. One of these times is the flight that brought me to Kunming. I'll bet he plans to sneak aboard a flight that's headed for India."

"How?"

"If Sun sneaks aboard undetected at night, he can hide behind the air compressor that oxygenates the plane. Even if he's discovered, they won't turn around. He may be a prisoner in India, but it's better for him there than here."

"We need to alert Colson. I need Sun captured here." Anya dashed out the door and headed for Colonel Colson's office.

FORTY-THREE

ANYA AND MAC WALKED INTO COLONEL Colson's office later that afternoon. He ceased shuffling papers and looked up. "You're not due to report for a few more days."

"Sir," Anya said, "we believe Sun, the man we're after, is planning to stowaway on an aircraft bound for India."

Colson lifted the phone receiver, but before he could dial, Mac pressed his finger down on the receiver button. "Let us handle the situation, Sir."

Colson shifted his eyes between them and then settled on Mac. "All right. I'll notify the Base Commander to be on the lookout, but to stand-down."

"This bastard is clever. Make sure they don't spook him. It may be our last chance to nab him."

Colson nodded and picked up the phone.

THE TWO ARRIVED AT THE AIRFIELD AN HOUR before sunset. Clouds loomed in the air with the possibility of rain.

They had positioned themselves in the control tower to get a better layout of the entire field. A hangar sat to the right of the landing strip, a pilot's shack to the left. Several maintenance crewmembers scurried about fueling an aircraft getting ready for takeoff while an incoming plane taxied down the runway.

Anya held binoculars to her eyes and surveyed the area. "Do you see him, Mac?"

"Not yet."

"Keep your eye on that plane ready to leave. I'm sure he is going to make a run for it."

A crewmember removed the fuel hose from the sitting aircraft. The flagman signaled to the pilot to prime the engines.

"Look toward the stern of the plane," Mac said.

"I see a crewman giving signals to the pilot."

"The rear, you landlubber."

"Oh." Anya felt her face flush. "I see someone walking toward the plane."

"I think that's our guy."

"I can't see his face clearly, but he's a lot shorter than the others on the field."

Mac put down his binoculars. "Let's go catch a criminal."

What little sunlight remained began to descend below the horizon as the two reached the airfield. The noise from the rotating propeller blades made audible communications impossible. Mac gave Anya a hand signal to go around one way while he headed to the opposite side.

Mac approached the C-46 Commando aircraft as if he were boarding along with other passengers. He spotted Sun dressed as a maintenance worker pretending to inspect the tail section. Sun turned his way. Both froze for a moment and stared at each other. Sun dashed toward the hangar with Anya and Mac in close pursuit. They reached the entrance and stopped.

"Wait here," Mac said. "Don't let him get past you." He drew his weapon and slowly made his way into the hangar. Cartons were stacked twenty feet high. He froze when he saw boxes marked dynamite. A dead guard lay on the floor. Mac stepped back just as a stack of cartons crashed inches in front of him. Mac turned on his heels and ran toward Anya.

"Run," Mac shouted. He grabbed Anya by the arm. They raced out of the hangar.

A loud boom rang out. Anya felt a force hurl her to the ground.

Mac leaped to his feet and helped Anya up. "Are you all right?"

Anya nodded as she rubbed a sting from her forearm. Several more explosions rang out. A fireball lit up the night's sky. The smell of hot metal lingered in the air.

"Do you think he's dead?" Anya said.

"Knowing him, he probably escaped out a window before he set off the dynamite. The guy has more lives than a cat. Go around to the back. I'll go this way."

Gun ready to shoot, Anya crept around the corner of the burning building. She heard sirens approaching as she reached the rear. The iridescent firelight silhouetted another figure, but it was too tall to be Sun. As it inched near, she saw it was Prune.

"Sun's here somewhere. I can feel him," Mac said.

Prune spoke to Anya.

"What did he say?" Mac said.

"He witnessed someone dart away from the hangar before it lit up."

"He's hiding out there somewhere." Mac pointed to the darkened field.

"Maybe the glow from the fire will help us find him."

"Fan out and let's see if we can flush him into the open. Check the ditches on either side of the runway where Sun could hide."

Prune took the right side, Anya the left, and Mac down the middle. The fire radiated light similar to twilight. Wild rabbits scampered across their path as the three crept forward.

Anya heard the plane engines rev as it headed for the strip. "It's going to take off. We'll have to abandon our search until they're gone."

The plane's engines accelerated as it taxied. Sun popped out from his hiding spot and dashed across the strip. Prune was on his tail like a lion after an antelope.

Mac noticed that Sun's gait looked different. "He's injured."

"I'll bet he could use some of that pain medication he stole." Anya and Mac moved out of the path of the aircraft as it careened down the runway—full throttle.

Anya watched as Sun ran toward the plane. "What's he trying to do, committing suicide?"

"I think he's going to try and stow away in the wheel well."

Prune raced after him from along the sideline. Sun stumbled. His arms and legs flailed as he tried to remain upright. He ended facedown on the ground, directly in the path of the plane's wheels. The aircraft started to lift. Sun tried to roll out of the way, but he was too late. The right front wheel caught his midsection, hurled his body into the air, before it smashed to the ground.

Mac and Anya dashed over to investigate. Sun's eyes were open. His breathing labored. He reached into his inside pocket. Mac jammed his pistol against Sun's temple. Blood spurted out of Sun's mouth as he removed his hand then his body went limp. A pinging sound hit the pavement. Anya stared at her red Asscher ring for a moment before she picked it up and slid it onto her finger.

FORTY-FOUR

ANYA LIFTED THE SHOT GLASS FILLED WITH A glistening clear liquid. She closed her eyes and downed the spirits. A burn hit the back of her throat like fireworks. Warmth permeated her chest. Comfort set in. Eyes opened, she stroked the rim of the glass with her tongue then reached for the bottle.

"You drink as though you were performing a ritual," Mac said.

Anya stretched her back. "I haven't felt this good in months." She pushed the filled shot glass toward Mac.

"A bit early, isn't it?"

"Vodka is mother's milk to a Russian. It's the water of life." She pushed the glass closer to him with an unblinking stare.

Mac took a moment before he picked it up and

knocked it back. He coughed uncontrollably before he could place the glass on the table. He pounded his chest to control the coughing.

Anya giggled. She glanced at her red diamond. The reflection of sunlight through the window made it sparkle.

"Why," Mac coughed, "do you think he gave back the ring?"

She shrugged. "Maybe, in the end, he wanted to atone for past deeds."

Mac slapped the wooden table with the flat of his hand. "He was a defect without moral conviction."

"Frankenstein's monster was said to be evil but in the end, he became a tragic hero." She knocked back another shot.

"What?"

"I'm not saying that Sun was a hero. But maybe like the monster, he didn't have healthy guidance in life."

"Sister, we are never going to agree on that one." Mac picked up the shot glass, filled it, and swallowed without a cough.

"Didn't you tell me once that a great shaman told you that sometimes you have to bend with the breeze or you'll break?"

Mac rolled his eyes at her.

"I suppose you'll go home now."

Mac leaned back in his chair and stretched out his legs. "There is nothing for me in the States."

"You have a wife and child."

Mac sighed. "Don't get me wrong, my wife is a good person." He paused. "And I tried to be a good husband and father."

"But?"

"For me—marriage is a prison—confining, mundane without excitement."

"And you need that intense stimulation."

Mac combed his fingers through his hair. "Sadly, yes. These last few days have been a refreshing holiday. I feel liberated."

"You remind me of my father—duty, discipline, and loyalty. You would have liked him, and I suspect the feeling would have been mutual."

Mac cocked his head. "What do you think of me?"

Anya snickered.

"What?"

"I remember the first time we met in that makeshift office back in San Francisco. You sat at your desk surrounded by file cabinets. I almost lost control when your pipe blew up in your hand. I thought, oh brother, this man is too stupid to run an operation. You were arrogant, rude, oppressive, offensive—"

"Okay, enough of my sterling personality."

Mac pursed his lips.

"But, I came to understand—to respect—that you were doing what a good soldier is asked to do. And in the end, you became my hero."

Mac blushed. "I wonder how the gangsters will manage, now that Colson has a good idea where to find them."

"I suspect Zhu's operation will collapse." Anya raised her glass in a toast.

The hum of voices entered the canteen. Several officers marched in, sat at a table, and ordered a round of drinks. A scowl crossed one of the officer's face when he spotted Anya.

"Don't worry about them. It's just the odor of condescendence," Mac said.

"I dare one of them to say something. I've earned the right to be here."

Mac chuckled. "Yes, you have."

Anya filled the shot glass, drank, and stared at the empty glass.

"What?"

Anya remained silent.

"Is there something on your mind?" Mac said.

She looked up. "I have lived most of my life in war. I have no real purpose without it. It gives my life meaning. I am, after all, my father's daughter. His life was spent on the service to his country." Anya fiddled with her ring.

"I know how you feel. It's not that we want this war, but there is something innate that calls to us."

"As though we were born at this exact time for this exact purpose."

"Colson should be happy," Anya said. Along with the medical supplies we handed over to him. He now has a full description of Zhu and several of his gang members."

Mac pulled a piece of paper from his inside pocket. "I received a telegram from Kevin."

"How's he doing?"

"He's making a full recovery and he got himself engaged to a socialite. He has a job waiting for him when he gets out."

"Glad to hear one of us has a plan."

"Yeah. The sorry S.O.B."

They both laughed.

"What do you think you'll do next?" Anya said.

"I've gotten so I like China.

"I know. I feel I found myself in China."

"I might just hang around here and see what kind of trouble I can find."

"I don't think you have to worry about that. Trouble seems to ride in your back pocket."

"What about you?"

"You forget. I report to Colson in the morning."

"Right." Mac rubbed his chin. "Mind if I tag along?"

"I just might be in need of a partner."

More about Red Asscher

P. C. Chinick is currently working on a Red Asscher prequel. The saga start in 1898 Russia and follows the story of Anya's parents, the revolution, and their escape to Shanghai. For release date information, visit www.redasscher.com.

CPSIA information can be obtained
at www.ICGtesting.com
Printed in the USA
LVHW010402040920
665076LV00002B/215